THE MESSENGER OF THE GROUND

JAN FORTUNE

Cinnamon Press
:: small miracles from distinctive voices ::

Published by Cinnamon Press,
Office 49019, PO Box 15113, Birmingham, B2 2NJ
www.cinnamonpress.com

Print Edition ISBN 978-1-78864-133-3

British Library Cataloguing in Publication Data. A CIP record for this book can be obtained from the British Library.

Designed and typeset in Garamond by Cinnamon Press.
Cover design by Adam Craig © Adam Craig.
Cinnamon Press is represented by Inpress.

Acknowledgements

Thanks to Adam Craig for listening to the first drafts of chapters as they were written. Thanks to John Barnie for his generous and meticulous editing. Thanks to Tamsyn Fortune-Wood, who urged this trilogy on. And thanks once more to the village of Tanygrisiau, where I lived for two decades, for providing the setting and the spirit of place.

THE MESSENGER OF THE GROUND

To Iris,
who is a force of nature and a gift

Part 1: The Glyndŵr Years

Prologue

When she comes round, her body is a single bruise blooming purple and yellows. She wonders how she has not already choked on the arid boulder of her tongue, her throat burns and, even in the thinning paleness of dusk, her eyes wince against the light. Cautiously, she sits, runs her hands over arms, legs, torso. Pain erupts from her permeable skin but there are no breaks, though she is not ready to stand. She pulls her legs under her chin, looking back towards Mytikas Peak. Two hundred million years in the making. How long had she existed there?

'Well, I'm done being your messenger,' she shouts into the landscape.

The meadows rise, bleak at this time of the year, the montane levels denuded of forest. Farther away, black pines huddle around the bodies of their logged siblings, the remnants of a forest that only yesterday had been green-scented, alive. She rubs her eyes, shaking her head like a horse flicking off flies. The forest should give way to Maquis shrubland across the foothills, but the land is pocked with charred craters, the earth rusted, the small trees and bushes brittle black skeletons. Higher still, the rock slopes are spattered white with snow and clouds, nothing unusual there. But the burnt shrub and decimated pines? How long has she been unconscious?

She stands cautiously. The sun is setting and a thick band of livid orange flames across the horizon between mountain peaks. Above it a thinner band of yellow shines beneath a deepening swathe of blue. The harsh biscuit browns of the rocks darken between pools of light that look molten. She turns her back on the range and scans the plain, shivering. One foot in front of the next, slowly, pain welling, not knowing where she is going, her mind fighting the idea that she has not only been violently exiled but that the world has changed in ways she cannot make sense of.

One foot in front of the next and there are no thoughts, only movement that slows and slows until she crumples onto the earth, unable to move, her mind a fever of images, names called over and over:

Arcus. Come back, Arcus.

Ninšubur. My name is Ninšubur, not Papsukkal. Why do you call me…?

Shine, Shapash, you are the torch, the lamp of the gods, the sun. You are Shapash, burning radiance…

Burning, her bones are burning. She feels her heart, her guts, fires erupting, her mind a cauldron of flame, names and images dissolving into one another, consuming her until…

On the burnt soil is a small bulb, the shape of a shallot or the single chamber of a heart, its onion-brown skin paper-thin. One iris bulb in a vast wasteland.

1

November 2077

Alys woke from her recurring dream. Always it was the day after Luke arrived in Y Tir and she was explaining operation Excalibur to him.

'So once Excalibur had done it's work, we loaded Glyndŵr,' she told him in her dream. 'It was a pity the inter-E-Gov communications and the defence documents were behind an extra layer of encryption, so we couldn't get to them. But we were most interested in being able to get to the Regulation Authority Database. We wiped all your files among other things.'

'Glyndŵr's like the history site I originally found you on?'

'It's actually multiple sites—history, ethical critiques of the Will to Govern, exposés of abuse. Glyndŵr generates endless copies of the sites' pages and randomly combines them over the top of existing sites or any site we've stripped out. So all the E-Gov citizen information sites and news sites, for instance.'

'Sounds complicated and brilliant.'

It was, but of course it was also only the beginning. In the two years between Dewi Jenkins getting Brussels' support for Y Tir to be recognised as a sovereign state and a member of the European Community, they had worked tirelessly with Luke and Emrys to develop Glyndŵr. Luke had a flair for story that went well with her maths and Emrys's magic, and all of it had been needed.

She edged out of bed into the cold of the November day and made her way to the bathroom. She leaned out of the window to watch Owain scattering feed for the chickens. 'I'll make tea,' she called. He raised a hand in answer, stamping to keep warm as he moved towards the house.

She passed the empty room behind the bathroom and touched her palm to the door as she had done every day since Taid died.

'You look glum this morning,' Gwen noted as Alys entered the kitchen.

'Thinking about Taid,' she replied. 'And about how little time we have to do something more permanent about the Hengst and Hunter sites.'

Gwen nodded. 'Kettle's on,' she said, as Owain entered the kitchen.

'Freezing!' He squatted in front of the log burner and jammed in another log. 'Dad's gone over to the Jenkins' to take the herbs for Taid Jenkins and see how Dewi is doing.'

Alys placed a large teapot on the table and Gwen set a rack of toast next to it. Owain was at the table in a stride, slathering butter on onto the hot, crisp bread before pulling out his chair.

'It'll be hard on Dewi losing Dafydd so soon after Betsan. And 77's no great age,' Gwen said, pouring three mugs of tea. 'Same age as my mam.'

'Nain's one of the last of that group now, isn't she?' Alys asked.

Owain looked up startled. 'But Nain's fine, right?'

'My mam is one of the fittest people I know,' Gwen said, smiling. 'But that generation went through too much. Pandemics and living in the mines and winters with not enough food. It's surprising any of them got to fifty with what they endured, and the amount of loss they had to live with. But there were some strong ones.'

'Like Nain Parry.'

'Super-strong. Angharad Parry was the generation before. Hardly any of them made it to old age.' Gwen took a long draught of tea. 'Right, who's for eggs? Or do you want porridge?'

'Porridge,' Alys said at the same moment as Owain called, 'Eggs.'

'Rock, paper, scissors,' Owain offered.

Alys laughed. 'Eggs are fine. Porridge tomorrow.'

'You going to Emrys's after breakfast?'

'Today and every day.'

'So is it industrial espionage now?'

'Pretty much—or at least that's the aim. Not that we want to exploit their corporate secrets. Just stop them.'

'But people don't seem to care what these companies do as long as they can stay entertained and have maximum convenience. I can't get my mind round that type of thinking at all.'

'It's not how you've been raised,' Gwen said, stirring dark yellow eggs into a moist scramble and adding pepper. 'And tags have changed people. They might call it human enhancement, but there's not much human in it at all, not as we've known it.'

'I just can't see the attraction of my memories and emotions being stored in a cloud where some hacker can hold them to ransom.'

'Me neither. But people who've lived under E-Gov can't see the attraction of having to remember dates and information or all the knowledge they need for work or of experiencing something once and then not being able to relive it.'

'But I can relive it,' Owain countered. 'I can sit here with a plate of eggs and see Taid across from me or be in the polytunnel and hear him telling me how to space the seedlings. I can walk up Moelwyn Bach and the scent takes me back to the time a big group of us spent the day swimming in the top lake, doing dives from the rocks. I can practically hear the splashes and feel the cold water and then the heat when we came out into the sun.'

'You're right, but if you'd never relied on your own brain to remember those things you'd have a lifetime of enhanced, full-sensory memories instead, with bells and whistles in more colour than exists in the real world. And if that suddenly disappeared, you'd be disorientated. Think how Luke was when he first arrived, even though he'd chosen to remove his tag.'

'Yeah, I know it's massive conditioning. I just hope that if I'd had that and then got the chance to go back to … well, to being myself, I suppose, that I'd choose this life. And if they all do it together then no one's at a disadvantage.'

'But these companies…' Alys shook her head. 'The chips they're about to produce go even further. E-Gov wanted control and tracking and I think the new regime isn't much better, but the tech companies are aiming higher—they want a complete end to private thought—every idea or even what you dream in your sleep is a saleable commodity to them.'

'But you'll stop them?'

Alys sighed. 'I really don't know. There's a growing clamour for access to the new tags in England. A lot of it in the Subs. People want what the rich already have and more of it.'

'But how would they afford it?'

'The big companies have gone with different models. Transense—'

'That's the Hunter's one?'

Alys nodded. 'Yeah, the "complete neurolife chip" they call it. That one is expensive. It's all about being exclusive and keeping the *hoi poloi* beneath you. But the Hengst's Enhanced Futures one, snappily called "Linkit" is going to be free. They—'

'Free? What like they're a virtual-life charity?'

'Not so you'd notice. The consumers don't have to pay because they *are* the product. Every scrap of the users' date is saleable.'

'And people will go along with that?'

'People will flock to it. The manipulations and invasion of privacy are all so intangible and the enticements are large—people who've scraped an existence in slums will suddenly be taking virtual vacations on tropical islands with every sense catered to. People whose lives are unremitting labour for a pittance will be able to escape to any hedonistic fantasy they want.'

'And they'll be more exhausted than ever,' Gwen put in.

'Sounds scummy,' Owain said, 'but why exhausting? They're just sitting there experiencing whatever distracts them from their real lives.'

'Because their body's will know it's virtual. The heart-brain and gut-brain won't be fooled. And because no matter how real it feels, it's always a distraction unmoored in time so it will leave them craving...not even knowing what they're craving for...'

'So they'll go back and back trying to find the satisfaction that's eluding them,' Alys added

'And feel more and more fatigue and craving, more and more alienation,' Gwen finished.

'That's hellish,' Owain said. 'Alys, you've got to take them down.'

'Thanks, brother. And meanwhile, we have to watch our own data. We think the supposed to be oh-so-shiny-clean new U-Gov has a whole covert department just aimed at taking our systems down.'

'But we're in the last stage of ratifying sovereign status with European protection. Wouldn't that be against international law?'

'Of course, but try proving it wasn't just some random hacker. We have to be beyond vigilant and make sure we're untraceable, which means planting more decoys than we feel we can manage some days. But the Mutineers have offered help and Zach and Saskia are learning fast, though I think Emrys and Dewi want them to take over integrating the refugees. They're so good with people.'

'The refugees don't seem like a happy crowd from what Gethin and Osian were saying.'

'I think a lot of the people who've left England for Y Tir thought we were some kind of rural idyll with cows that milk themselves and lambs that dance through flower meadows before laying down as tasty ready-cooked dinners. We don't live up to the montage in their heads. And in fairness, the housing stock is probably worse than they've left behind in the Subs, and really dire for those who were in the Centres. Porth may have great views but it's been empty for a long time and it's hard work putting those houses right.'

'Do you ever regret breaking the code?'

Alys paused. 'Some days, certainly some moments. But we've given people a chance to choose a different way for humanity to develop. Maybe they won't take it in the end, but I still hope they will.'

Owain nodded. 'Well, another month and we'll be a wholly sovereign state. We both got what we wished for, now I suppose we have to find out what the wishes mean.'

Alys grinned. 'I suppose we do.'

Iris: the messenger

Once, being a messenger felt like the world was falling at my feet. I was the gods' bridge to the world, and to the underworld too. The gods' words were mine to carry as I shape-shifted through place and time. I was Iris, goddess of rainbows, carrier of words. Trusted and powerful, rainbows spilled from my coat, rain poured from clouds I seeded with ocean storms. Oath-breakers were lulled to sleep by the waters I carried from Lethe. And the caduceus was mine.

But the earth withers. The people are starving. They no longer sacrifice to us. Zeus begs you …

Then tell Zeus to return my daughter.

She ate willingly, Demeter, she…

The roar that could have split rocks open stopped my words. Demeter would not be persuaded and so the year was divided into seasons, the darkness holding sway when Demeter's daughter spent six months of each year in Hades.

The look of disbelief before the howl of rage when I told Menelaus that Helen had eloped with Paris. No atrocity would be enough to staunch his bleeding pride. So much blood would flow from that moment…

And I was there for all of it, through all those years at Troy, carrying messages from Zeus, changing shape to be heard by Hector or Helen, to instruct and warn Hector and Achilles alike.

I carried Aphrodite to safety when Diomedes wounded her.

I travelled through sea to find her sisters in the ocean cave, swam on their tide of tears to Achille's side, to comfort him. Swift as air, I brought the winds, Boreas from the north and Zephyros from the west, to ignite Patroclus's funeral pyre.

I impressed Poseidon with my understanding of justice and was the small voice guiding Priam.

And when my sisters, the Harpies, ceased their storms, I'd soothe the world with rainbows. I even turned back Argonauts who would have harmed my unloved Harpy sisters.

Though I was born of Thaumas and Electra, Zeus was my father through those years.

I could move through Hades as easily as through water or air, on golden winds that carried light. Swift-footed, shifting shape, no height or depth was beyond my reach.

2

Zach cupped his face for a moment, then looked into the man's face. 'Thing is, mate, this isn't the Centre, but I can get someone to come and show you how to get started, help you get into it.'

'Plumbing?' The man looked like Zach had suggested he take up python wrestling. 'I'm a film director. I... Surely there must be... well, not robots, but... these people here, they're more used... I'm just not...'

Zach resisted the urge to suggest the film director was not used to finishing his own sentences and nodded sympathetically.

'Film director, eh?' Saskia had come to stand behind Zach.

'Yes, you might have heard of me. Seen my work. I...'

'We haven't had much access to films,' Saskia interrupted, her voice quiet but firm, 'but maybe you can show us.'

Zach shot her a puzzled glance.

'Luke and Alys need a lot of content for their sites, trying to give people an idea of the benefits of an unhooked life. Maybe you can help them,' she looked down at the paperwork on Zach's desk, 'Mr Grant?'

'Well, yes, but at the moment... we've got all these

leaks and the, well the toilet…'

'So how about Zach finds someone to help get your waterworks moving and I let Dewi know you'd like to donate your skills?'

'Dewi?'

'Mr Jenkins is the President of the Gader.' She watched the puzzlement flicker across his face. 'The Council if you like, but more like an assembly of those who represent what they hear from all of us.'

Mr Grant nodded.

'So what do you say, Mr Grant?' Saskia asked.

'Yes. Yes, I'd be glad to help.' He paused. 'Did it take you long to adjust when you got here? I mean I'm assuming … you don't sound Welsh…' he trailed away again.

'We came from Telford Subs, mate,' Zach put in. 'This place is paradise by comparison, far as I can see. You didn't want to stay in England even with U-Gov in power?'

Mr Grant shook his head. 'It was a big decision, but within months we could see U-Gov cosying up to big tech firms like Hunter and Hengst. I've got a good friend in the civil service. He reckoned the party was getting a lot of donations that way. And not transparent either.'

'The companies developing Transense and Linkit?' Zach asked.

‘That’s right. I could see it’s only a matter of time before we’re all chipped again, not by mandate, but the only way to be cutting edge enough to hold down a job or get a qualification or enjoy leisure. And these next generation nanochips are going to make what E-Gov had look like nursery toys.’

‘It’s a really brave decision,’ Saskia said, smiling.

‘It wasn’t easy. I wake up every morning wondering who I am without all that instant access to so much knowledge, so much culture…’

‘Yeah, as long as it was knowledge and culture they wanted you to have.’

‘You’re right, but it’s still like losing several limbs. I feel brain fog all the time. I know it sounds ridiculous, but the thought of trying something as alien as plumbing feels like total overwhelm.’

Saskia pulled a chair towards Zach’s desk and sat down at eye level with Mr Grant, putting her hand on his arm. ‘I think nearly all those who’ve left the Centres are talking about brain fog. Maybe we should get some groups going, share experiences, help people flex their own brains and memories? Maybe you could make a film about the transition?’

‘Genius, babe,’ Zach said admiringly. He turned to his client. ‘Okay, Mr Grant. You tell Saskia what you’re going to need and she’ll set up a meeting with the Gader. In the meantime, I'll get a couple of Messer friends to help me look at your plumbing. This evening good for you?'

'Really? Thank you. Thank you.' Mr Grant stood and held a hand out to Zach who shook it. 'And call me Seb. Sebastian Grant.'

When Seb had left the small office in what was a long-disused sport's centre, Zach hugged Saskia to him. 'These people, babe, they're all at sea. It's like they have to learn everything about life from scratch again. I think the ones from the Subs like us are having the easier time.'

'Yes. I don't suppose they had a clue how hard it would be even after two of years without their tags. There's still a lot more technology and the XRverse to hide in back in England. But the last couple of years must have been pretty chaotic and they're still going through brain fog.'

'Collateral damage,' Zach said. 'There's a whole country out there full of people wondering where most of their mind has gone. I know it had to be done, but it's pretty heavy.' He gave Saskia another quick hug. 'Thank goodness we were so disadvantaged in our former life, eh? Anyway, I'd better see the next person.'

'Me too. I only came in for more pens. I just couldn't resist helping that guy.'

'Glad you did.'

Saskia grinned. 'I'll send in your next victim.'

The woman who entered was tall and elegant. She took a seat across from Zach and held out her hand.

'Claudia,' she said, 'Claudia Mason.'

Zach shook her hand. 'Zach Hindmarsh. And what's brought you here today?'

'I'm looking for Luke Malik. I was his pod-carer in Birmingham. And a friend of Nazir's—and Vivian when she was alive.'

'Wow. This is turning into quite a day. How long have you been in Y Tir, Miss…'

'Claudia. You can call me Claudia. I arrived last night. I held out while there were still young people in my pod who I'd cared for over years, but a lot have gone back to families now and then one of them went missing, a good friend of Luke's…'

'Kyle?'

'Yes. Is he here?'

'He is.'

'I'm not sure what skills I can offer. Good admin, I suppose. But there's nothing in my past that seems real anymore, so here I am.'

'You've been assigned a place to stay?'

'Yes. On the harbour. It must have been a lovely place once, so I'm hoping it will be again. And the views of the water and out towards Cnicht are beautiful.'

'Any brain fog?'

Claudia tilted her head and considered. 'That's an interesting question. I think all of England's Centres have gone into collective brain fog since the end of '75. But people cope differently. Most are holding out for reconnection via the promised Transense. And until then they're living inside the XRverse as much as possible to keep from thinking. I suspect that those trying to explore what it might mean to be a none-enhanced human are probably already in Y Tir or suffering in silence.'

'The extended-reality-verse is better than brain fog reality, eh? I once heard someone say the true definition of spirituality is to be able to distinguish the real from the unreal.'

'Interesting thought.'

Zach nodded. 'You're the second person today to mention Transense. I sometimes wonder if Emrys and Alys think they broke the code for nothing but they always say the point was to give people the choice, even if not many want to take it.'

'It's good to have the choice, yes.'

'And as to your skills, my girlfriend, Saskia—you saw her on your way in—she's thinking of setting up groups for people from the Centres to try to find ways to cope without the XRverse and facing all this brain fog. Sounds like you've managed a lot of groups of people going through changes working as a pod-carer.'

Claudia smiled. 'I've done some counselling courses and spent a lot of time sitting at a table over a hot drink with tissues on hand. I may just have found a new niche.'

'Excellent. And your address is…'

'6 Oakley Wharf.'

'I'll let Luke and Emrys know where you are.'

'I'd love to surprise them.'

'Oh, well—they're in Rhyd. Follow the road up round Llyn Mair and past the Tan y Bwlch railway station. It's just a handful of cottages. It's quite a walk, mind, or the train goes twice a day.'

'I've watched the steam train from my window. When did it restart?'

'Just a few months ago. It was for tourists up to the '20s. Alys said her granddad used to talk about going on it at Christmas when he was a boy and in the summers they had jazz concerts at Llyn Mair and then cocktails on the train. It's a good communication link, right down to Blaenau.'

'Will the other one re-open?'

'They're thinking about it. Only Beddgelert has had houses occupied till recently, but now there are people beyond that, all the way to Caernarfon, so it would make sense. There aren't many vehicles except farm ones and we want to keep it that way.'

'Well, I've got a neighbour with a bike who says she'll

let me borrow it so I think I'll give it a go. Thank you, Zach. And keep me posted about the groups.'

'I will.'

Zach leant back in his chair and closed his eyes. He'd seen a lot of people today, but the last two were intriguing. A lot of refugees ended up going back to England, especially those from the Centres, but he thought Seb and Claudia would make it here. Now to get some food before rounding up a likely crew to help him with Seb's plumbing. Sufficient to the day as far as the desk job went, he thought, but when he opened his eyes a young guy about his own age was stood in front of his desk.

'Woa!' Zach jumped. 'Didn't hear you come in, mate.'

'Stealth,' the guy quipped. 'I'm Moriaen. Moriaen Hunter.'

'Take a seat, Moriaen. Hunter, eh? Like the tech tycoon who…'

'Not like,' Moriaen cut in. 'I'm Harrison Hunter's son. Illegitimate. Black. Everything he can't stomach. And I want to stop him.'

Iris: the coming of the usurper

It was my rainbow that connected the gods to their worshippers on earth. And the caduceus was mine.

And then he was born.

Zeus was my father, if not biologically, then spiritually. And I was good at what I did.

Hermes with his winged feet flew no faster than me with my golden wings. I had once led souls to the afterlife, had moved in and out of ocean, sky and underworld, shapeshifting as I went. But I was diminished after he arrived, reduced to being the go-between for Hera at best.

When Odysseus sailed from Troy on his ten year sojourn, it was Hermes who carried Zeus's messages to him. It was Hermes bearing the replica of my caduceus, as though it was his own invention, as though I'd never existed.

Once, at Zeus's command, I had carried a ewer of water from the River Styx, to put to sleep all who perjured themselves. But after Hermes usurped my place, Hera wanted me as the lackey of her petty spite. It was me that she sent to pluck out a strand of Queen Dido's hair so that she would die and go to Hades. It was me she sent, in the shape of a Trojan woman, to incite the Trojan mothers to burn Aeneas's ships so that they could not leave Sicily.

Ovid tells how, after her husband died and became a god, Hersilia pleaded with the gods to let her become immortal as well so that she could be with her husband once again. Juno, as Hera was known in Rome, heard her plea and sent me down to her. With the touch of a single finger, I made Hersilia immortal, transformed her into a goddess so that she could join Quirinus, deified by Romulus on Olympus.

But it was always only another mission on Juno's behalf.

We could have been brother and sister, this trickster with his shamanic shifting between the visible and invisible worlds, who gathered to himself the personas of divinities before him. He could have been Thoth to my Sheshat.

But Hermes paid no attention to me. And my father had forgotten me.

3

January 5 2083

Alys shivered as she turned over, waking slowly and feeling the pull to hunker further under the covers of their little bedroom in Bwthyn Heddychlon. She had been an early riser all her life until the last few months, which had stirred a deep desire to hibernate.

'Peppermint tea,' Luke offered from the bedroom doorway, holding out a tray. 'And sourdough toast with eggs. I thought you might be hungry.'

Alys smiled. 'Ravenous.'

Luke set the tray down on the bed and slid under the blankets next to her. 'How many are you eating for exactly?'

'One and he's a dragon,' Alys said, grinning and lifting a slice of buttery toast to her mouth. 'I'm off to Ty Meirion after breakfast,' she said between mouthfuls. 'I offered to help Mam with the cooking for tonight. Saskia and Zach are making red pea soup and Moriaen is doing that amazing lemon almond cake, so me and Mam are on the main course. How about you?'

'I've got a few tweaks I want to make to the last film on Glyndŵr before the gathering. Seb's helping me with it.'

Alys wrinkled her nose.

'They're good people, Alys. The Scots have always resisted the colonialists just like the Welsh and…'

'It's not about them being Scots. It's… these particular people… They say all the right things, but there's something… I'm not sure what it is, there's something off with them.'

'They've been a lot of help so far and they need help protecting their country while they get their independence.'

'I realise they should have their autonomy, but even with it… well, the EEC isn't anything like it was when we joined. They may not have officially bought into e-governance in the way U-Gov did—faster than blinking—but they're still sliding towards it. I know we did it to give people a choice but I'm pretty shocked that most people can't see what's in front of their faces.'

Luke nodded. 'We're always going to be a minority written off as the lunatic fringe, but…' He hesitated. 'You know, maybe not always. I still believe things can change—not just in Y Tir or the Highlands, but generally. I still think that at some point all this stuff will come crashing down and people will want to be, well—human again.'

'You've seen Hunter's latest advert?'

'Yeah, they don't even pretend to be slick anymore, just utterly cheesy—*Don't just get any life, get a Neurolife—you know it makes Transense.*'

Alys stuck two fingers into her mouth and feigned a gagging motion. 'Quite, but people are still buying it over there in La-La U-Gov land.'

Luke slid out of bed and nodded. 'I know, and they're not the half of it. It's a miniature step from hanging out in the XRverse as much as possible to getting fitted with Hengst's little gizmo.'

'All for free.'

'Or people think it's for free. If you're not paying for the product, you are the product. Damn, Alys, I need to keep believing in this.'

Alys smiled. 'Sorry, I know it's hard to keep the faith. Go and get your shower. Are you working with Emrys on Glyndŵr?'

'Yes, and Moriaen's joining us later too. I suppose after cake-making duty. He's got another idea for infiltrating Hunter's system.'

'Tell Emrys to keep an eye on those Picts for me. I know I'm not just being paranoid.'

'We'll all keep an eye, but I hope it's just hormones speaking. We could do with the allies.'

Alys threw a pillow in Luke's direction. 'Cheeky toad! Hormones! My intuition is sharp, Luke Malik. Now get out of here. I've got time to nap before I get ready for a big day of cooking.'

'See you at Capel Horeb then.'

Luke blew a kiss across the room and Alys returned it before snuggling under the blankets.

In the huge upstairs mezzanine of Capel Horeb, Claudia and Kyle were busy laying the long table with greenery, cutlery and glasses when Alys arrived with the cooking group.

Claudia hugged each of them in turn. 'Dewi's already here,' she said, 'he's down in the office with Emrys and the boys.' She turned to Zach and Saskia. 'This smells amazing.'

Zach shrugged. 'All Saskia's work,' he said with pride. 'I just chop and stir to order.'

'Rubbish, Hindmarsh. You're a better cook than me. I'm still learning after all those years of microwaved slop.'

'Well I have no idea how anyone gets kidney beans to taste like the most fragrant, spicy bowl of heaven,' Claudia put in.

'My Jamaican family on the net. Every one of them unchipped.' Saskia pushed back ropes of dark hair and smiled. 'But not as fragrant as Moriaen's cake. Is he downstairs?'

'Yes, deep in conflab with Luke, Emrys, Dewi and Cei

before our guests arrive.'

Alys put a large dish on the long kitchen counter at the back of the room and swayed slightly.

'You alright, cariad?' Gwen was at her side.

'Bit light headed is all. I'm fine.'

'Go and sit down. You've been on your feet all day.'

'Can I bring you anything?' Claudia added as Alys curled into the corner of the seating area.

'Water? Fruit juice?' Saskia asked.

Alys smiled. 'So many mams. I'm fine, really, but water's good.' Downstairs, a bell rang. 'Oh, they're early,' Alys said glumly.

'It might be your dad with Owain and Seren,' Gwen said.

'Or Gethin and Osian,' Claudia offered, handing Alys a glass of water.

'No, it's the Picts,' Alys insisted, noticing the look of concern pass from her mam to Claudia.

Alys listened to feet on the stairs and Emrys appeared ahead of the three Picts. 'Everyone, let me introduce Eoganan Ogilvie, Carvorst Caltram and the enchanting Aislinn Mael,' Emrys said, his voice the theatrical performer of Nazir Malik.

He put his fingertips together and made a characteristic bow. Alys noticed Claudia blanch for a moment before moving forward, hand outstretched to greet the guests. Enchanting? Alys mused. Enchanted. Emrys is enchanted. She began to stand to greet the group, but Aislinn was already at her side, her hand on her shoulder.

'Don't get up for us.' Aislinn's voice was silken. Her dark red hair fell across her face as she held Alys in place. 'Such a beautiful ring,' she said softly. Alys had an urge to hide her hand as Aislinn leant in closer and whispered, 'I've always wanted to meet the bearer of the ring of Eluned the Fortunate. The most powerful of all the Treasures of the Island of Britain. Invisibility can be such a strange gift, though, don't you find?'

Aislinn stepped back and Alys looked down at her right hand. On the middle finger, just above her knotted gold ring with its small red stone, a line of blood sprang fresh and red. Alys stood, swayed and…

When she came round, the gathering was in session. She could hear Owain talking fast, a sign that her brother was in full political-mode. She caught words—*U-Gov, EEC protocol, unhooked autonomy*—but couldn't make sense of the sentences.

Next to her on the cushions, Claudia hunched over a bowl of read pea soup. She smiled as Alys's eyes flickered open and put a finger to her lips.

'Are you okay?' Claudia whispered. 'Your mum couldn't find anything wrong except that scratch. We thought we'd just watch over you. Was it her?'

Alys startled. 'Aislinn? You think she's… I don't know, but there's something…' She kept her voice as low as Claudia's but Aislinn turned.

'Oh, Alys, thank goodness.'

'Don't crowd her,' Gwen instructed, pushing in front of everyone as they rose to check on her. All except Aislinn, who remained in her seat, smiling, and Emrys, who sat still, gazing at Aislinn.

Alys closed her eyes. Eluned and Myrddin Emrys had no need of electronic enhancements to sense each other, but today Myrddin's mind was shrouded in fog, unreachable.

Aislinn finally stood and came to Alys's side with a glass of red liquid. 'Hibiscus tea,' she said, holding out the glass. 'So refreshing.'

Alys sniffed nervously, the slightly acid pomegranate scent of hibiscus. Still she nursed the glass, not drinking.

'A drink will do you good, Alys,' her mam said.

Alys sipped nervously. 'Sweet,' she said, 'hibiscus is usually tart.'

'A little liquorice and violet,' Aislinn reassured her.

Alys sipped again. She was thirsty and the cold tea delicious. She drank the glass. 'More?' Aislinn asked, moving back to the flask she'd left on the table. 'I take it everywhere with me.'

As Alys finished the second glass a chant played through her mind:

Scotch broom and yarrow to bleed on the morrow,
Mugwort and wormwood, to flush the babe downward,
Pennyroyal, rue, angelica too, to hasten the blood
so you'll rue this day soon.

Alys shook her head, as though she could dislodge the song she'd never heard before.

'Can you eat, Alys?' Luke was crouched at her side, holding out a hand. She stood unsteadily and allowed herself to be shepherded to the table. She glanced around the assembly as they went back to eating and talking, Luke still solicitous at her side.

Across the table, Seren glanced up from feeding Gwion and smiled. 'This'll be you soon,' Seren said. 'The best sleep draft in the world.'

Alys smiled at her sated baby nephew, now deeply asleep.

'When will the baby be born?' Aislinn asked.

'May,' Alys said. *No it will be sooner than that*, a voice in her head whispered.

'Are you okay, Alys? You look ever so pale,' Claudia

said.

Alys watched the gathering glance at her, some trying not to be obvious. Gwen had warned them not to fuss and crowd her, but she could feel their concern—Saskia and Zach, her brother and Seren, her dad, Dewi and Cei at the far end of the table apparently in deep conversation with Eoganan and Carvorst, cast continual furtive glances her way.

She nodded. Talking felt like such an effort.

Gethin moved towards her. 'Me and Osian are off home. It's a fair cycle back to Rhyd for old codgers like us. If you want an early night we can see you home, cariad.'

Alys looked towards Luke. He bit his lip. 'I should stay really,' he started. Alys nodded again and smiled, but a well of loneliness gaped inside her. Emrys is the only one who hasn't asked how I am, she thought, looking across at her mentor, who seemed not to have taken his gaze away from Aislinn since he'd introduced her.

'Thank you,' Gwen said to Gethin and Osian. 'That sounds like an excellent idea.'

'I could come with you,' Claudia added. 'I was going to stay here tonight anyway. I can camp in your spare room if Luke's going to be late home.

'Thank you, Claudia,' her mam spoke for her. 'That's really kind. I'll call first thing in the morning to make sure all's well, but hopefully a good night's sleep...' Gwen paused. 'How does that sound to you, Emrys?'

Emrys seemed to surface as though from deep under water. 'Sound?'

'Gethin and Osian are going to see Alys home and Claudia will stay with her. We were thinking that some of you might be talking long into the night?'

Emrys looked around the table. He's taken no part in the conversation with Eoganan and Carvorst, Alys thought. He's being kept out of the discussion by her.

He blinked. 'Yes,' he said as though he wasn't sure what he was assenting to. 'Yes. Claudia and Alys.' He turned back to Aislinn.

Gwen pursed her lips and ushered Alys and Claudia downstairs.

Gethin and Osian followed. 'I don't have your insight,' Gethin said quietly as they moved into the atrium of the chapel, 'but something's not right here, is it?'

Alys threw her arms round him. 'He's enchanted, Gethin. I've been telling Luke for weeks there's something wrong about all this. He seems to think I'm being racist against the Picts, but you're right.'

Osian whistled softly. 'Can we do anything?'

'I don't know. I can hardly think in here. She's… I'm not sure what's she's done to me, but…' Alys saw her mother's face tighten in anxiety. 'I'll be fine, Mam. I think I'd better get out into the air though.'

Gwen nodded, not looking convinced, and Claudia hugged her. 'I'll take good care of her, Gwen'

'Thank you. All of you.'

From the top of the stairs, Aislinn's voice said softly, 'I just wanted to say goodbye, Alys. I so hope this passes quickly.'

'She'll be fine,' Gwen said, a little too curtly. She turned her back on Aislinn to hug each of them and bustle them into the crisp January air. Go carefully all of you. She stood outside on the step and dropped her voice. 'Can you two stay at Alys's too? I'm not even sure why, but…'

'Yes,' Osian and Gethin said together. 'Good not to be too far from all this anyway.

'There's only one spare bed,' Alys said anxiously. 'The other spare room is full of computers and books'

'Geth and Osian can have it. I'm good on the sofa,' Claudia reassured her.

'Or you can come in with me? I don't think Luke will be back tonight,' Alys said, trying not to let the tears show in her voice.

The spasm of cramps made Alys cry out as she woke. She felt the warm gush of blood follow the pain. Claudia was awake instantly.

'Oh, darling.' Claudia pulled back the covers.

There was a knock on the door and Alys nodded as Claudia glanced at her. 'Come in,' Claudia spoke in a rush as Gethin opened the door. 'Can you get Gwen?'

'Of course.' Gethin was gone.

Alys curled into herself, sobbing as another contraction expelled a liverish clot.

Claudia looked up to see Osian in the doorway. 'Geth'll be back soon. Would a hot water bottle help?'

Claudia nodded. 'And pads. Period pads. And towels. Have a look in the bathroom.'

Alys looked up as Gwen came into the room. Her mam looked grey, she thought. 'I'm sorry,' she said.

'No, cariad. It's nothing you've done. I've got Gethin making some cinnamon milk. It'll help with the pain and… help move things along.'

Alys watched her mam trying not to cry.

'Thank you.' She steadied her voice. 'Is he already dead?'

Gwen nodded. 'Probably, love.'

'Will I see him?'

Her mam nodded again. 'Most likely. He'll be about 10 centimetres by now. But it might take a while. Sometimes days, occasionally longer, but it can be fast too.'

'It was Aislinn's tea,' Alys said, panting as another contraction swept her into its pain. I heard a chant:

'Scotch broom and yarrow to bleed on the morrow,
'Mugwort and wormwood, to flush the babe downward,
'Pennyroyal, rue, angelica too to hasten the blood
'so you'll rue this day soon.'

'Well, those are all abortifacient,' Gwen confirmed.

Later, after the tiny infant emerged, his translucent, softly downy body fitting into the palm of her mother's hand, Alys let Gwen bathe her like a baby, then wrap her in the freshly changed bed, a mug of herb tea at her side.

Alys lifted the cup and sniffed.

'None of the herbs Aislinn used,' Gwen said. 'You'll keep bleeding for a while but hopefully not so much now. This is to help you sleep. Valerian, chamomile, lemon balm and passionflower. I'll be on the sofa downstairs if you need me. Just shout—Gethin and Osian will hear you too.'

'What about Claudia?'

'She's in the kitchen. She can go and sleep at ours or...'

'Can she stay in here with me?'

'I'm sure she can.'

Alys put down the drained teacup and huddled under the covers.

'Oh, Alys, I'm so sorry.'

'You weren't here.'

'I know, love. I'm sorry. It was just so important that I see the whole meeting through, we…'

'More important than our baby?'

'I didn't know, Alys. I can't stay with you every second of the day and night just in case… I'm sorry, love. We can get pregnant again. There'll be another…'

'What? Our baby has just died… They're not replaceable like lost socks, Luke.' She could hear her voice getting louder.

'I didn't mean it like that, but… well it's not even four months yet. Aislinn was saying after you left how common miscarriage is with first pregnancies. How it usually means there's something wrong with the baby, so…'

'Luke, sweetheart…' Claudia began gently.

'I'm not sure this concerns you,' Luke cut her off. 'I'm not even sure why you're here. You're not my mother. And by the way, my father isn't interested in you—'

Alys winced at the spite in Luke's voice, a tone she'd never heard from him in the ten years since he'd come to Y Tir.

'Surely even you could see how taken he is with Aislinn?' Luke continued.

'Luke, I think you should leave now.' Alys tried to keep her voice low and steady.

'What?'

‘I don’t want you here right now. Go and stay at the chapel—or anywhere.’

‘I…’

‘I think Alys is right.’ Gwen stood in the doorway to the bedroom. ‘She needs a bit of time, Luke.’

Luke stomped from the room.

‘He’s not himself,’ Alys said softly to Claudia. ‘And nor is Emrys.’

‘She’s right, Claudia.’ Gwen added. ‘It’s not real, this spell that Aislinn has cast on my brother. I don’t have the same magic as him and Alys, but I have enough to know when we need protection.’

Gwen moved towards her daughter, sat and wrapped her arms round her, cradling Alys as their tears began to flow.

Iris: the unravelling

Happiness, sadness, grief, love, jealousy, wrath… the gods of Olympus felt it all. They felt it with a magnitude that distant mortals could never have imagined and they had the power to act it out with a terror that no human torturer could ever have dreamt of. The gods I dwelt amongst were not restrained by the moral codes handed down to mere humans, for us there were no social norms, only the rule of power and unconstrained emotions.

Children so often have no idea that their home is strange, dysfunctional, a haven for sadistic bullies whose injustices can only be endured. It's only with retrospect—when they've encountered other families—that they begin to think that what they knew as home was never a sanctuary.

It was like that amongst the gods. And it was a big family, a cacophony of egos and volatile emotions where the smallest provocation could become thirst for revenge, the catalyst for bizarre torments.

Think of Io, expelled by her father when Zeus took an interest in her, turned into a heifer in Zeus's attempt to conceal his affair from Hera. Io ended up driven mad by the stinging gadfly Hera sent to torment her, swimming seas and oceans in an attempt to find peace. Hera never visited her rages on Zeus, always on the unfortunates he seduced or raped.

Think of Lycurgus who banned wine from his kingdom and outlawed the cult of Dionysius. When the god threw a party on Mount Nyseion, Lycurgus went in swinging an axe and Dionysius had to find shelter in a sea cave with Thetis. But Dionysius was the god, not Lycurgus. The revenge taken on the mere king was terrible. Cursed with insanity, Lycurgus, who'd ordered all vines to be cut down, saw his own son as though he was a vine, and hacked him to pieces, first pruning him—ears, nose, fingers and toes. And still Dionysius's rage was not sated. He cursed the whole of Thrace with barren land so that the oracle advised the people to kill their king. But mere killing was not enough—he was bound and thrown to a man-eating horse, which tore him to pieces.

Think of Ixion, spinning across the heavens eternally on a wheel of fire for behaving towards Hera as Zeus behaved to all his conquests.

What did I expect then, when I said no to Hera, when I challenged Hermes? That they would realise how unjust they had been and repent? That I would be Zeus's darling adopted daughter again? That Hermes would break his caduceus in two and promise not to carry one unless I agreed?

It wasn't that I expected any of that. I was like the rest

of them and thought no further ahead than my latest wild emotion. Like them I was volatile, greedy, a narcissist looking for my next emotional high that was never enough, and then the next…

I was a god, but dispensable. Hermes more than filled my place. No cults followed me. I had become a pretty story of rainbows and wings for adolescent girls. So when I began to throw challenges and tantrums, what followed was inevitable.

I remember very little of my unravelling. There is an image of flames, an echo of pain that I carry always and then, there I was—hundreds or thousands of years of suffering later, a bruised and bloodied body on the arid plain, looking back towards Mytikas Peak. I had no idea how long I had existed there, how long my torture had been, yet even in that moment my bravado had not left me: *I'm done being your messenger,* I shouted into the emptiness.

But the gods, however far back in history they had become, had not done with me. I tried to hobble away, but collapsed onto the earth, images of other selves burning my mind more than the invisible flames that were consuming me:

Arcus. Come back, Arcus.

Ninšubur. My name is Ninšubur, not Papsukkal. Why do

you call me…?

Shine, Shapash, you are the torch, the lamp of the gods, the sun. You are Shapash, burning radiance…

I burnt with each of the gods I had lost or had ever been…

4

Alys watched Luke trying to fold clothes into a bag. Ten years since he'd worn the expensive smart fabrics that marked the privileged in the Centres of E-Gov, and still he couldn't fold a shirt.

'It won't matter, Luke,' she offered. 'Emrys will make you appear smarter than all their dazzling executives once you're in their offices. And enhanced too. It'll feel strange for you having mind-links again, even if it's only from Emrys's magic. Will you be okay?'

It was the longest sentence she'd spoken to him since Brân had died, but he didn't seem to notice the effort.

'I'll be fine.'

'Will she be there?'

Alys wished instantly that she hadn't asked.

'She has a name, Alys. Aislinn is as powerful as Emrys. She's our most valuable ally and I won't have...'

He stopped. He looked flushed and uncomfortable. Alys had an urge to challenge him, ask what he wouldn't have, but she knew the answer. He wouldn't tolerate her accusations against Aislinn the enchanter. She'd heard too many times in the last few weeks how important this allegiance was, how powerful Aislinn and the Pictish sage, Carvorst Caltram, were; how generous their leader

Eoganan Ogilvie was being. Of course she would be there, haunting Emrys, who had said less to Alys than she had to Luke in the two weeks since the gathering at Capel Horeb.

'Do you want me to fold those for you? I thought we could…'

'I'm fine doing it. Like you say, it won't matter if they are crumpled old bits of linen. Emrys has it covered.'

Alys took a deep breath. 'I was going to suggest that when you're done we could walk down to the…'

'I don't have time, Alys. Anyway, it's mawkish.'

'Mawkish?'

'You were going to suggest we visit its grave, weren't you? It's ghoulish. It wasn't a baby, Alys, you need to come to terms with that. Aislinn says nature flushes away foetuses that are malformed, that weren't meant to live. You need to move on. You shouldn't have buried it, shouldn't have given it a name, my mother's name for pity's sake!'

His voice was shrill and his colour high. Alys wondered where the Luke she had known had gone. She wished she hadn't told Luke that Brân meant 'raven', his mother's surname, a gesture to those they'd lost and to the coming together of their families.

'Okay, Luke. Well, I'm going up to the lake. You'll be gone by the time I get back. Go safely.' She paused. 'And when you get back, you might want to go stay in Capel Horeb or… somewhere else. I can't do this with you for the moment.'

'What the…' his voice exploded as Alys twisted her ring, covering the small ruby and disappearing from his sight.

'And no, Aislinn won't be there in fact!' Luke shouted at the empty room.

'She'll come round, Luke. She's been through a lot and Gwen says the bleeding hasn't fully stopped yet. All these mad thoughts about Aislinn causing the miscarriage are just grief talking. Give her some space. When she sees how much the Picts are contributing to the effort she'll come round. Of course she will.'

'I suppose,' Luke replied to his father. 'I've just never known her so irrational.'

Emrys, who Luke still thought of as Nazir Malik, smiled and put his finger tips together. 'It's probably a good thing that you'll be away for a while. Now, I think I hear Moriaen at the door. We need him to hold things together here with Alys out of action and then I need to brief you on how the spell of enhancement will work.'

'You already did.'

'Again then. It's going to be disorienting, Luke. Remember how long it took to get used to not being tagged and plugged in? Well suddenly you're going to seem to go back to it, but it will take all my energy to maintain that while your in Hengst's lab and the Hunter's offices.

'Isn't it a bit weird that they have actual buildings with desks and people coming in and labs on the premises?'

'Hengst only has a skeleton staff in person to copy-cat Hunter. Harrison Hunter thinks he's being ironic with a full in-person workforce producing tags that ensure no-one has to do anything in person themselves. He's actually an unhinged overage-teenager in a suit, with a lot of money and power.'

'No wonder his son was such a great person to be around at school,' Luke commented.

Emrys grinned. 'Quite. Still, it was probably your fight with Bradley Hunter at school that started your journey here, so he's more than played his part. Though I suspect he's got more to play in this. He's cleverer than his father, more calculating and not as juvenile.'

Luke nodded. 'So the offices are just for show?'

'Show, irony, because he can make people who never need to leave home turn up when he decrees, reminding them how valuable neurolife is… The man's a narcissist with toddler tendencies.'

'Will Moriaen be able to maintain Glyndŵr and keep the guerrilla sites churning out while we're gone?'

'I think he will. But he'll ask Alys if he needs help. I know she's grieving and things are difficult for you with her, but she is still Eluned and Creirwy, goddess and shapeshifter. As you witnessed only this morning.'

In Birmingham, Luke felt instantly disoriented before Emrys had even begun to rehearse the neural enhancement with him. His cover would be as an international journalist from the Lebanon, urbane, rich and eager to offer Hunter and Hengst a profitable introduction to a wealthy region. He would be Nazir Ahmed. They checked into The Grand Hotel, their suite providing a view across the cathedral and farther across the city. Travel and hotels had picked up business in the first years of U-Gov, but with the move back to a virtual life, and new generations of neural enhancements for the rich or unwary, as well as the lure of hiding from reality in the XRverse for everyone else, hotels had become novelties again. Real travel was for the ultra-rich, people like Nazir Ahmed and his elusive bodyguard, known only as Saqr. Only the richest, most lavish hotels could survive. Even in countries that had treated neural enhancement with caution, most work, social life and play revolved around virtual spaces provided by the companies presiding over the XRverse.

Luke and Emrys settled into a palatial suite surveying

the Centre. Already Luke felt shaky and hoped his father wouldn't notice. They'd walked from the station that Luke had begun his flight from almost ten years ago, despite the effusive protests of the station guard that they should take an electric car along with their luggage. But Emrys had waved away the man's warnings.

Corporation Street was wide and empty. The buildings that had all been shops now stood vacant or were dormitories for menial workers, those whose labour was cheaper or more novel than the army of robot-gadgets. It was only when they'd got to Temple Row that a few real shops survived amongst the financial institutions that were mostly empty facades housing computers. These were the shops where the richest and most entitled could be fitted for clothes, not by the invisible mechanisms of virtual fittings, but by human hands; an elite fashion. The hands of those living in the miserable dormitories and schooled to feign interest in nothing but those they served.

They crossed the green around the cathedral to Colmore Row and entered the hotel, instantly surrounded by the sycophancy of the exquisitely trained hotel staff, each perfectly on-script thanks to the ever-watching free enhancements that were advertised as a major staff privilege.

'Hunter models,' Emrys had already set up a mind-link to Luke, inaudible to any network. 'Still in the experimental stage. So much for privilege.'

They slumped into the sofas in Luke's room.

'I feel a bit nauseous,' Luke confessed.

Emrys nodded. 'I'm not surprised. Why don't you get a shower and I'll order some food up here. Then we can go through tomorrow's interviews when we're a bit more settled.'

Luke stood and opened his bag, taking out his toiletries, though he had a feeling a lot more would be provided in the bathroom. 'Yeah, that sounds good,' he said. 'Do you think any of your installations are still on display in this Centre?' he asked, as the bathroom door slid open in front of him.

The laugh was pure Nazir. 'I somehow doubt that.'

'Okay, so we have the first interview tomorrow at Hunter's. I'll be in the atrium. They will let you bring your bodyguard that far. You need to make sure every question you ask sounds as fawning as possible while getting them to tell you as much as you can. And ask to see everything.'

'They'll scan me?'

'Of course.'

'They'll see their top of the range model. The one that isn't being tested on hotel staff and posh-shop workers.

The one with all kinds of ingenious spyware sold as the cutting edge in health monitoring but giving them plenty of data on your spending, thoughts and probably bowel movements for all we know.'

'Nice. But they won't see any of that for real in my case?'

'No, they'll see the stream I've created. Shallow, rich, thinking about his next meal, thinking how cool these guys interviewing you are, thinking about going through the motions of this job cos Daddy really wants to buy into Hunter's and get the goods for his cronies and become even richer.

'Your real thinking is what I need to hear, so concentrate. It's going to be exhausting, Luke, for both of us.'

'More exhausting than I knew possible,' Luke confirmed the next evening as they walked away from Hunter's Transense Lab, housed in the building that had been the Museum and Art Gallery, and had overlooked Nazir's most famous installation.

'Yes, but you did well.'

Luke grinned. 'I could eat any amount right now. Could we eat out of the hotel? That place is too perfect.'

'I think that could be possible,' Emrys said, smiling. 'There's a restaurant on Temple Row that screens its customers. Bookings strictly by wealth.'

'Sounds awful. But as long as the food is plentiful, I'm in.'

'The food is famous and another place with the novelty of real waiting staff. So *de rigueur.*'

At the table, Luke was too lost in his menu to notice how hard the waitress was staring at him. He took a sip of water as he looked up and choked on it, spurting liquid across the table.

'Luke?'

'Sorry?'

'Luke Malik?'

Luke watched the look of panic on Emrys's face. He tried not looking directly at Katie, the girl he'd been besotted with, the girl he'd got into a fight with Bradley Hunter over, the girl who didn't associate with 'darky messers'.

'Ahmed, my name's Ahmed,' Luke said, avoiding using 'Nazir'.

Katie shook her head. 'You look just like someone I knew.'

'Is all well with your table Miss Lomax?' A tall woman with steel-grey eyes stood behind Katie.

'All is very well,' Emrys said confidently. 'So much choice. Miss Lomax was taking the time to describe some of your dishes.'

The steel-eyed woman looked suspicious but only inclined her head. 'Excellent,' she said. 'Let me know if I can do anything further,' she added as she left their table.

They ordered quickly and Katie, flushed and nervous, blinked into the eyepiece of her XRset as they rattled off dishes.

Luke wished they could leave, but Emrys mind-called him to keep calm. 'The restaurant can't trace us, we're too important. And anyway, discretion is their selling point.'

'You mean they provide more than food?'

'Much more.'

At the end of the meal, as Luke went to the bathroom, Katie appeared at his side. She darted a hand towards him, tucked a scrap of paper into his hand and was gone. Luke uncurled the fragment of paper in the bathroom stall. *Please help. Cathedral Square bench. Noon tomorrow.*

Emrys was waiting for him in the doorway when he emerged. He smiled at the tall manager, thanked her profusely and ushered Luke into the street. 'You can't meet her, Luke.' His voice was quiet, final.

'What… I… That's really intrusive!' he blurted finally.

'I know and I'm sorry, but we don't know what's going on here or who Katie has become. We can't jeopardise what we're here for.'

'Aren't we here to stop all this misery of corporations owning people and no privacy?' Luke heard his voice becoming too loud and looked around anxiously, but the street was empty.

'Yes, but not one sad story at a time. Where would that get us?'

'I was just one sad story when I ran to Y Tir.'

'Perhaps, but you took that into your own hands. And it was your destiny. You don't get to be Arthur by rescuing one damsel in distress. You're here to bring the light back to the world.'

Luke's shoulders slumped. 'It's too much, Dad.' He couldn't remember when he'd last called Emrys 'Dad', even when he'd known him as Nazir.

'It's always too much, but we still do it.'

Emrys put an arm round him as they walked towards the hotel, releasing it as they came in sight of the gliding doors.

'Welcome Mr Ahmed. Welcome Mr Saqr.'

In the suite, Emrys jumped as he opened the door with a flick of an eye. 'Morganne?'

Morganne ran into his arms, weeping.

Emrys held his half-sister and Luke could see that he was shaking. He gently edged himself away from Morganne and stroked a strand of dark hair from her wet face. 'Gerhard?'

Morganne nodded and Luke watched all the air go

from his father's body. He fell on his knees and Morganne followed him, holding him, the two of them rocking and keening.

'Less than an hour ago,' Morganne told him when they were finally seated in the sofas in Luke's room. 'Laurent wanted to come instead of me, but I needed to do this.'

'I knew he was ill. And I knew he was lying about just how ill, but…'

'We're never prepared,' Morganne agreed. 'I wanted to come before but he insisted your work had to come first.'

Luke pictured his grandfather, his mother's father who he'd only met since joining Y Tir, and then only occasionally. Yet even those brief meetings had affected him deeply. There was a kindness and wisdom in Gerhard that steadied those around him. And he'd heard the stories of how Gerhard brought Emrys to Y Tir and had been so important in saving it repeatedly in the darkest of times.

'You need to go to the funeral,' he said simply. 'I wish I could go with you but…'

Emrys looked up, a little dazed. 'Of course I want to go, but Gerhard wanted…' Emrys trailed away. 'I just gave you a lecture on how we can't save the light one sad story at a time and now I'm the one jeopardising the mission if we have to postpone these interviews. We might not get another chance like this.'

Morganne shook her head. 'My little brother was always a slow learner, Luke,' she said, smiling for the first time that evening. 'That's utter tosh, Myrddin Emrys. Sometimes one sad story at a time is all we have the power to change and it's a ripple. It all matters. We can't start pitting the big stuff against the small stuff. In fact, we shouldn't even be constructing these hierarchies of big stuff and small stuff. It's the good we can do. That's it.'

Luke looked at Morganne and began to cry.

'Luke? Luke, it's okay,' Emrys said, still in confusion.

'No, it's not. I've completely blown it with Alys because I got so damn big-headed with the importance of my destiny while she was grieving for our baby by herself. I've lost her because I might talk big about caring for one sad story when I meet someone I haven't seen in a decade, but when it really mattered, I was an emotional moron.'

Morganne rose and sat next to Luke, putting her arms round him. 'We all make messes, Luke. You and Alys will be fine.' She stroked his head. 'You catch on quicker than the genius, your dad, anyway,' she quipped, lightening the mood.

'So it's decided,' Emrys said, not sounding certain still. 'I'll go back with Morganne and Isabelle will support you here.'

Luke looked anxiously at Morganne and Emrys. He'd heard of François, Myrddin Emrys's maths tutor when he first went to the Mutineers to hone his skills in maths and magic, but…

'She's amazing,' Morganne reassured him, picking up his uncertainty. 'The magic seems to get stronger with every generation in that family. Isabelle's mother, Heloise, took over from Armelle as the healer and midwife and now both her children, Isabelle and Louis, are powerful mages and shifters. You'll be in good hands, Luke.'

'She'll look like me moving around the hotel or going to the interview,' Emrys added. He paused. 'I'd like to ask someone to come with me,' he said, turning to Morganne. 'Her name's Aislinn. She's one of the Pictish allies, also a powerful mage. I'd like…'

'Of course,' Morganne said, putting a hand on her brother's arm. 'I didn't think there would ever be anyone else after Vivian.' She smiled. 'She sounds wonderful.'

She glanced at Luke, who grinned. 'It's fine. I love her too, though not like Emrys. I just wish Alys did as well.'

Morganne looked interested. 'Alys doesn't like her?'

'She thinks Aislinn gave her something that caused the miscarriage. It was just hibiscus tea. She drinks it herself all the time. But it's got mixed up with the grief somehow.'

Morganne said nothing.

'You'll adore her, Morganne,' Emrys added.

Morganne nodded and smiled.

'Will you go straight away?' Luke asked, needing to break the quiet.

'I think so, but only if you are okay alone tonight.'

'I'm fine. I'm so tired all I'm going to do is sleep.'

'Good. Stay in the hotel and order food here tomorrow. I've re-arranged your next interviews for the day after so just sit tight and Isabelle will be here by tomorrow evening.'

'I know. I'll be fine. Really.'

'To the hotel it will look like I'm still here. I can keep that up for tonight and tomorrow as long as I'm not having to move with you too much.'

'Can I go for a walk? There's something about this place…' Luke looked at his father uncertainly.

'No, stay inside. I know it's weird, but so is out there.'

Luke nodded reluctantly, wondering how he could meet Katie and hoping Emrys wasn't reading his thoughts.

'They'll only see me with you if you stay in these rooms,' Emrys added. 'They'll ask questions if you go out alone.'

'Okay. I understand. Now you two should go. I'll probably sleep all night and most of tomorrow after this anyway.'

Alone, Luke sat pondering before picking up the XRglasses and flicking to the concierge. If he left the hotel, would Emrys know? Most likely, but he couldn't stop him. But that was only half his problem. The hotel would see him going out alone. That could start a whole chain of questions and problems…

'I need a favour,' he began. 'It's a personal matter. Can you send up your head of security? But please tell him to be careful not to wake Mr Saqr.'

The knock on Luke's door was barely audible. Luke rose and opened it, grateful that Emrys had left him the mind-ability.

'Julia Worthing,' she said, entering the room. 'I'm told you need some assistance, Mr Ahmed.' The head of security was probably in her 40s. She looked like a pod-mother, efficient but not what he had expected.

'It's rather personal, maybe it's not a good idea… I…'

'Our discretion is complete, Mr Ahmed.'

'Thank you. It's just. My bodyguard…' he glanced towards the door of Emery's empty room. 'He's very protective. But I met someone today. Someone I know. He doesn't want me to see her again, but… If you could message me to say my brother is in the Centre and wants a private meeting, then he'd let me go alone.'

'I'm sure you're already certain this… meeting would

be safe, Mr Ahmed?'

'Yes. It's someone I was at school with. We were close. Lost touch.' He stopped himself, he was saying too much. He didn't have the skills for this.

'And your guard wouldn't help you to effect this meeting here? Your friend would be most welcome. Surely your guard is here to help ensure your safety, not your choice of friends?'

He couldn't say that Katie would trigger their sensors, that she was unconnected. The silence lengthened.

'He's a bit… He's known me since I was a kid, I suppose. He was there when my mother died… I know he's kind of overstepping the mark, but he's been in our family so long and…' He was making this worse.

'I completely understand.'

Luke nodded gratefully. He wasn't sure he'd made any sense that could be understood. This was harder than escaping school and Birmingham.

'What time would you like your call and what information do I need so it can be overheard?'

Luke smiled. 'Thank you,' he said.

'I didn't think you'd come,' Katie said, as Luke sat down next to her. She looked like the Katie he'd known, the pale oval face and straight brown hair, but she looked so tired.

'It wasn't easy. I had to give my … er, bodyguard the

slip.'

Bodyguard? And eating at Luxuria. You've come a long way since doing a runner and causing a national sensation. Did you really kill that Regulator?'

Luke shook his head. 'No, but I suppose I have come a long way. How about you?'

'Can't you see for yourself?' There was more exhaustion than bitterness in her voice, Luke thought.

'Sorry. Do you want to tell me about it? You said you needed help.'

'I do. Can we go somewhere private?'

Luke glanced back at the hotel and she followed his gaze.

'You're staying at the Grand? Wow! Well you can't get me in there. I know somewhere. You need credit but that's no problem for you. The restaurant uses the place for its clients. Don't look like that, Luke. You can't have got as rich as you seem and still be as naïve as you're making out.'

'Is it far?'

'Two minutes away. Cherry Street.'

Luke sat in the bathroom of the guest-facility wondering who he was. He'd just spent the last two hours in bed with a woman who'd once rejected him because she was a racist, while at home his wife was still bleeding from the miscarriage of their baby. He wiped away a tear and looked at himself in the mirror.

'I've always wanted to do that,' Katie said as he emerged from the bathroom. 'At least since my dad disowned me after your pathetic Standing Ground mob broke the E-Gov codes.'

Luke shook his head. Katie's voice had changed. 'I don't understand,' he said.

'I want to tell you a story Luke. It won't take long.'

Once there was a man called Morfryn Nazit Malik. A powerful man. Some say he was a demon, others that he was some kind of magician. A genius anyway, but not someone who knew much about fidelity. He fathered a child in France, I've heard, someone as powerful as him, but her mother died and the story has it that, heart-broken, he just had to keep fathering children by people who could never measure up to the lost love of his life, Igraine.

This Morfryn Nazir Malik fathered your own father—Nazir Malik, the darling E-Gov celebrity artist who disappeared at the Winterval festival the year you ran away from school. There were probably other children too, but the one I know about was called Jasmine, your dad's half sister. Unlike your father, Jasmine didn't rise to fame. She was left to rot in the Subs, impoverished and ageing fast. But while she still had her looks, Jasmine had an affair with an older man from the Centre. It was a bit of sport back than—finding some docile lover in the Subs and pretending to be daring by leaving the Centre for the affair. People weren't chipped then so I suppose it was mildly risky. Anyway, inevitably Jasmine got pregnant and the rich guy took pity on her. He generously bought her baby and gave the girl a new surname (not his own, of course, she had to find that out for herself later).

Now what would he want with this mongrel girl? He never allowed her any home visits, but she was in an exclusive pod and an exclusive school and had the finest implant. And it was through this that she was groomed to befriend, and as she got older, more than befriend, a boy in her pod and class. Bradley Hunter, heir to one of the two giants in the tech-industry. Why did her father care so much about Bradley? Because his own empire was the rival giant, Hengst Futures. The girl's father was Ross Phillips. He used his mother's surname. His father was a Welshman, one of your crowd I believe, Ifor Tigaen.

And the girl? He called her Katie. Katie Lomax. And she grew up like a princess till the son of Nazir Malik, who'd done so well for himself, unlike poor Jasmine, made sure that Katie would be thrown on the rubbish heap just like her mother. With the code broken and the chaos that followed, Katie was of no use to the nice Mr

Phillips. So here she is, the daughter of your father's sister. Does that count as incest, Luke? They're so complicated, these family trees, aren't they? It's pathetic as revenge goes, I know, but it's the best I could manage.'

Luke ran to the bathroom, throwing up before he could reach the toilet. When he came out, Katie had left.

Iris: falling through myth 1

Arkē. Come back, Arkē.

My sister, *Arkē,* betrayed us. Why would anyone fly from the company of the gods to join the Titans? Why would my rainbow sister, the mirrored arch in the sky, so beautiful and intelligent, take sides with Kronos? A cruel tyrant who overthrew his father, proclaiming he would bring justice, only to use his power to throw his brothers into the abyss of Tartarus, to be tortured eternally. A beast who ate his own children in an effort to prevent a prophecy of his doom becoming true. Only my father, Zeus, his youngest child, was saved by his mother, hidden in a cave and raised by the goat, Amalthea.

It was Zeus who forced Kronos to vomit out his swallowed children by mixing mustard in his wine; Zeus who led the war against the Titans of Mount Othrys; Zeus who divided the world with his brothers, Poseidon and Hades.

But during the war my sister left us to side with these monsters. Monsters! Yes, but what of the Olympians? I woke screaming her name for hundreds of years, sick with the thought of her suffering in Tartarus, yet never blaming the hero Zeus who had thrown her there.

Now my own body burnt with fever. I felt the pain

he'd inflicted on her, my back aching with the torn flesh, the way my sister's must have burned when he tore her iridescent wings from her body, ceasing her flight, ripping her identity from her. He gave my sister's wings to Thetis as a wedding gift, and Thetis gave them to Achilles, to wear on his feet. Podarkes some called him—feet like Arkē.

Who will he give my golden wings to?

Arkē, you chose one nest of vipers, I another, and both of us have been cast out and torn apart.

5

Luke walked briskly thought the reception area of the hotel wishing he had Alys's ring. Could people see what he'd done? Emrys was using energy to maintain a cloak of inane chatter in his mind so that the staff would see him as connected, but he must look guilty, surely? And a mess. He could still taste the vomit.

The door to his room slid open at the blink of his eye and he startled.

'You must be Luke? Isabelle—Isabelle Martin.'

She was around his age, dark haired and blue eyed. Luke thought her voice was cold.

'Emrys and Morganne told me you'd be here all the time so forgive me if I seem curt. Perhaps I misunderstood.'

'No, sorry… I… I needed to walk. This place…'

'Just so you know, Luke, I'm not reading your mind, but I can tell when I'm being lied to. We're going to need to work together better than this.'

Luke said nothing, flailing for words that wouldn't come.

'You look like you need a shower. Shall I order some food while you're in the bathroom and then we can start over?'

Luke nodded, feeling feeble.

Isabelle listened with an impassivity that Luke found more unnerving than anger. Was she judging him? Why wouldn't she? Not content with emotionally abandoning Alys, he'd now been unfaithful to her, and with Katie Lomax.

'Katie said she was taking revenge,' Isabelle said slowly when he finished.

'Yes, she…'

'And she just happened to be your waitress at pretty much the only restaurant Emrys would think it was safe to take you to?'

'Yes, but… I mean she couldn't have known we'd show up… How could she?'

'You have a traitor in Y Tir. And if I'm right, Ross Phillips knows you're coming tomorrow. He's not giving an interview to an unknown Lebanese journalist…'

'Well, not absolutely unknown, Alys and Moriaen planted a lot of stories across the net and my profile is good—aristocrat with all the connections Phillips needs to break into the Middle East and keep up with Hunter.'

'And Moriaen is trustable?'

'With my life.' Luke knew he meant it and Isabelle nodded.

'This Ifor Tigaen. He has no possible relatives left in Y

Tir? It was a pretty bitter fight between him and Myrddin Emrys, after all—a battle of dragons.'

'There was just him and his mother. She died before he left. The only other relative that people in Y Tir knew of was a brother—Iwan. Ifor was using him to fence Y Tir's medical supplies into South Wales and the Midlands.'

'And no one knows what happened to him?'

Luke shook his head.

'The traitor's likely to be someone in the Gader and even more likely someone involved with Glyndŵr. Who would that be?'

'Emrys and Alys do all the heavy maths and magic and Moriaen helps—he's not got their magic but Emrys reckons his maths is second only to Alys. Gethin and Kyle are the other coders—both really good for mere mortals, but it couldn't be Gethin. He's probably more loyal to Y Tir than Emrys. His grandparents were practically the saints of the place. Angharad Parry died the year I arrived. She was 97 and kept on teaching and serving on the Gader right up to the last couple of years. Her husband was the doctor who trained Alys's grandmother, a hero of the first pandemic. Died looking after people who got sick. That just leaves Kyle. We were in the same pod from toddlers. Definitely not him.'

'Who else?'

'No one else does that level of tech. The coding stuff

isn't my strong point, but I produce most of the content for the guerrilla news sites—the continuation of the Glyndŵr virus that Alys and Emrys launched after Excalibur had done the code breaking work. And then there's Seb…'

'Seb?'

'He was a refugee. Arrived around the same time as Claudia…'

'Who is?'

'She was my pod-mother in Birmingham, before I ran away. She's on the Gader now. She's a counsellor and…'

'Trustable?'

Luke nodded again. 'I was really cruel to her before I left for this trip. She took care of Alys when…' he paused to steady his voice and Isabelle put a hand on his arm.

'So this Seb?'

'He's a film-maker. He went to the settlement office where Zach and Saskia were working to get help with his housing when he arrived and struck up a conversation about how he'd been a film maker and he'd got out because he could see it wouldn't be long till everyone was tagged again, this time "voluntarily" so they could compete at work or just get through life.'

'And he offered his services to make films for the Glyndŵr sites?'

'Yeah, he's really good and…' There was a long pause.

'I need to get some water,' Luke said, standing and going to the fridge in the room's console. 'He said all the right things.' Luke sat down heavily and took a long drink. 'He was full of stories of how U-Gov was cosying up to big tech firms like Hunter and Hengst. He said he had a friend in the civil service who'd told him U-Gov ministers were getting big bribes as well as party donations to speed up rules on testing the next generation nanochips on "volunteers". He just said everything we needed to hear to make us…'

'Trust him?'

'What now? Do we go to the interview?'

'We need to be sure that your traitor is Seb, of course. Who else is on the Gader?'

'Dewi Jenkins has been leading it for at least ten years now, keeps trying to give up but he's good. Solid and calm in a negotiation. He got Y Tir's autonomy recognised with the EEC, him and Alys's dad, Geraint. There's Alys's brother—Owain. He used to be pretty hot-headed but he's mellowed a lot. Then Claudia and Seren—she's Owain's wife. Alys's mum trained her as one of the doctors and Seren's there on protest to represent them—Gwen's not one for political meetings. Oh, and Cei, that's Dewi's son, a farmer. And Saskia and Zach. They rescued me when I was running from Birmingham. They lived in the Subs but came to Y Tir soon after me. Zach can fix anything. He's not so fond of the meetings but he puts up with them. Saskia trained as a teacher and works with Leuci, Cei's sister.'

'You'd trust all of them with your life?'

'Yeah, I would, but…' Luke shook his head. 'Back in the days when they were hiding out in caves they had someone betray them. One of their own, so…'

'So you have to wonder and check everyone out. Anyone else on the Gader have a husband or wife who could be the traitor?'

'I'd rather not wonder about anyone,' Luke said despondently. 'Gethin's married to Osian. He's a forester and his mother was on the Gader way back. Seb's definitely the only one whose background we don't know anything about so the only one who's likely to have some link to the Hengst empire.'

'You know Claudia's background? Or Zach and Saskia's?'

Luke's colour rose. 'No, but… It can't be…'

'I'm not making accusations, Luke, just saying there's a lot to consider. How old is Seb?'

'About Emrys's age—two or three years younger maybe.'

'The right age to be Iwan Tigaen's son if he'd had one, which would make him Ross Phillips's cousin.'

'I've been working with him for nearly eight years. It

just seems crazy. He's playing a long game if you're right.'

'Battles of dragons are very long games.'

'I'm not sure I'm up to this.'

'Ah, but you are, Artu.'

'Artu? I'm not… I'm just myself. I'm just Luke, not a shapeshifting mage like my dad or a goddess like Alys. I'm not even like you—able to shift here and take on Emrys's appearance to the hotel staff and fake being tagged… I'm no one.'

'Artu returns whenever we stand our ground, Luke, and he's never a mage or god. He's a leader.'

Luke ran a hand through his hair and took a deep breath. 'You're saying I should do the interview?'

'I am. They won't harm you. They want information from you as much as we do from them.'

'What if I mess it up? Give something away?'

'If you cancel, they'll know you suspect something. They may not know what exactly, but alerting them could lead to a worse mess. Your people need to do more digging into Seb's background before he's warned and bolts, if it's him.'

'I've got no choice then. And I'm going to have to tell Emrys about Katie, aren't I?'

'You mean you thought you could hide that from him?' Isabelle laughed. 'You have met your father?'

Luke emerged from the interview feeling not only exhausted, but contaminated. He cast a questioning glance at Isabelle as he came into the lobby of the office, housed in what had once been a whole shopping mall. She made the slightest of nods and began to walk to the door. Outside on the balcony she made another slight nod and pointed to the escalator. They passed a chain of smaller offices downstairs, keeping their silence, and out into the street, walking briskly towards Cathedral Square. Luke could feel his heart pounding. Had he messed it up?

'You did great,' Isabelle said at last as they neared the empty arcade that led into the square.

'I did?'

'That was a long connection for me to maintain. I'm starving. How about you?'

'Famished, but don't suggest eating at Luxuria.' He wished instantly he hadn't mentioned the place.

'I think we'll stick with the hotel.'

Luke showered while they waited for the food to arrive, needing to wash the day away. Ross Phillips was a man in his late fifties, impeccably dressed, smug and with a way of saying things what sounded like compliments but were calculated to undermine and unease. There was something sly about him, an oily cunning that left Luke feeling unsettled even in the flow of hot water. But

Isabelle had said he'd done great. He hoped she'd meant it. She didn't seem like someone who would dissemble.

He heard the food being delivered while he was drying in the flow of warm air he'd switched to after the shower. He smiled, thinking how he used to take such technology for granted.

'Ah, there you are, we want this hot. Smells amazing. So fragrant,' Isabelle said. 'We eat well at home, but somewhat more simply. This is pretty special.'

She passed a fork through a mound of pale yellow rice flecked with slivered almonds and pomegranate seeds, and grinned.

'I'd love to bring Alys to a place like this. She'd be amazed,' Luke said, sitting at the table as Isabelle began to fill a plate with rice and mirza ghasemi.

'Have you eaten this before?' she asked.

'Nazir used to make it when I had home visits. Aubergine, tomato, egg, and garlic—he used those a lot.' Luke paused. 'I haven't called him Nazir for years, but there are things he does that make me think of him as that. He's different as Emrys somehow, but the same as well, if that makes sense.'

'It does.'

'Did I really do okay in there?'

'Better than okay. He's a wily fox, that one, but you were good at deflecting his barbs.'

'He knew I wasn't Nazir Ahmed, though, didn't he?'

'Undoubtedly. He also knew about your… encounter with Katie.'

'That was the part where I nearly choked,' Luke admitted. 'So she's still in touch with him. The whole thing was set up… Katie was planted.'

'Yes, which means they have a lot of inside knowledge. It also means they don't care that you know Phillips is Ifor Tigaen's son. They must feel really confident that you won't make any connections to a traitor in your camp.'

'They may not realise we know about Iwan. It was a really brief chance meeting, apparently. Dewi's dad took a group of young people to do a raid on a medical supplies depot and there he was—Ifor's twin, who was supposed to have died back in the second pandemic just as E-Gov was getting going. Dying had obviously been a cover story so Iwan could get into E-Gov and be ready to fence Y Tir's supplies. Emrys worked hard trading tech skills with places like Ireland and Hungary to get those. Anyway, Iwan mentioned that Ifor was dead and there wasn't really a reason to lie about that. Seems like Ifor didn't survive long after he fled from Y Tir.'

'Long enough to father Ross Phillips, but it sounds like you're right. He's feeling extra smug because he knows who you are and thinks you have no idea that we suspect Katie is not the abandoned waif after all, or that we might be looking for a spy. Well, that's some good news.'

Luke woke with a feeling that he was being watched. He looked around the room, then shook himself. Getting paranoid, he thought.

'Not at all, just finely tuned senses.'

Luke jumped and looked again, pulling at drapes and peering under the bed. No one. There's no one here, he told himself.

'Will you help me, Luke?'

'Aislinn? Is it you? I can't see you?'

'I know, but you don't need to worry. It's me. I'm in danger, Luke.'

'How?'

'Claudia.'

'I… I don't understand.' Luke sat on the bed feeling dizzy.

'The poison… it wasn't my tea, Luke. Claudia had already given Alys water before I arrived at Capel Horeb and then she went home with Alys. She must have given her something. It's Claudia who's betraying Y Tir, not Sebastian Grant. And she wants to poison Emrys against me too. She's been working on getting his trust, and more, for a long time, and I've spoiled her plans. I couldn't go to the funeral. Claudia got word that Emrys had asked me to accompany him and I needed to stay hidden from her.'

Luke put his head in his hands and wondered if he would be sick again. 'But…'

'Please believe me, Luke.'

'I do. I mean… It's just… Claudia isn't… She doesn't have your skills, your powers… How could she…'

'I'm not invulnerable. She's isolating me. I need you to save our alliance and to save Alys. Claudia has already turned her against me and she will do the same to you because you defended me. And Gwen too. Claudia isn't a mage but she has Alys on her side and Alys is more powerful than me. Together they'll turn Emrys against me soon.'

'I wish I could see you.'

'I can't stay, Luke. And please, tell no one that I've asked for your help. I'll make contact again when I can. You will help me?'

Luke rubbed his head. He felt faint and desperately wanted to go back to bed, to sleep for a long time. 'Yes. Yes, of course.' His voice sounded distant to him and he laid down, not bothering to get back under the covers.

When Luke woke again Isabelle was sitting by the bed.

'Yesterday really did wipe you out then?'

Luke opened his mouth, but shut it again.

'Are you feeling ill?'

'No, no, just exhausted.' So Isabelle didn't know about the visit. Aislinn must be more powerful than her. Of course she is, he thought.

Isabelle laughed. 'You get a guilty look every time you think something you don't want me to know,' she said.

'No… I…'

'You don't have to tell me your private thoughts.'

'I had this weird dream… I… I don't want to believe it, but it was like I was being told that the traitor isn't Seb, it's… I think it's Claudia.'

'Your pod-mother? Have you had prescient dreams before?'

Luke shook his head. 'It was so strong, though, and I… I suppose I've been thinking about Alys's miscarriage. I'm certain Aislinn didn't give Alys anything that could have harmed her. Emrys trusts her completely. Everyone loves her except Alys and Claudia. And Claudia was with Alys the whole time. She made her a drink before she went to sleep, before the bleeding started.'

'That's pretty heavy stuff. No wonder you look so washed out. Would Claudia know enough to pass information to Phillips?'

'Potentially. Not as much as Seb, but his films are pretty damning of Hengst Futures as well as of Hunters, so maybe that's another clue that it's not him. She'd know enough. Like you said, I don't actually know anything about her background, just what I knew of her as a kid.'

'Well, we've got a day to wait. Emrys will be back tonight and then I'll leave you to your investigations. You've got a lot to unravel before you even begin to think about ways to get deeper into the bowels of Hengst Futures.'

Iris: falling through myth 2

We are held in myth. We who are divine, who give our stories to the world so that the world has meaning. But what happens when we are exiled from our own stories? Who will he give my golden wings to? Will my story still be told? I am Iris. Even exiled, I am Iris.

But I feel myself falling, as though through myth, falling through story after story until I reach the floor of the desert where there are only ashes.

I am Ninšubur. My name is Ninšubur, not Papsukkal. Why do you call me Papsukkal? I am Ninšubur, vizier to Inanna and to An, the messenger of the gods, but messenger belies my power.

What I requested the gods gave. What I advised, the gods enacted. It was me who fought with Inanna against Enki, and who pleaded for her release from the Underworld when Enki held her prisoner. I was worshipped in cities from Lagash to Nippur, from Shuruppak to Uruk; the personal deity of the kings of Lagash. I was the mother of the land and bringer of healing, the guardian angel of those mortals who called on me, bestower of blessings.

And then he came to replace me.

Papsukkal. The lowly messenger. No one took him into their homes as their personal god. No stories of him remain. Yet his shadow eclipsed my bright body.

After hundreds of years my name no longer sang from people's hearts. There was only Papsukkal. Dull and functional, yet filling my place.

So Iris gave way to Hermes.

And Ninšubur to Papsukkal.

So I fell out of one story into another, out of the next story and into…

6

Seren stood and began to pace as baby Gwion's agitation rose to a wail. She began walking faster, jiggling Gwion, but the crying became louder. Saskia got up and held out her arms.

'Feel free to tell me to back off, you're the mum, but maybe he's picking up your tension?'

Seren manoeuvred the baby into Saskia's arms, where he began to settle as his mother slumped back into her chair. 'I can't take all this in.'

'None of us can, cariad,' Owain agreed.

Dewi shook his head. 'We've been through some dark times here, but this… Where do we start, Luke?'

Luke swallowed hard. 'Well, we're fighting on a lot of fronts. Ross Phillips isn't just interested in dominating the Connexions market with his new generation of nanochips that he intends will rival Hunter's Transense. He's out for revenge against Y Tir. He holds us responsible for his father's death.'

'I remember that day when me and Lowri ran into Ifor's brother. It was me who gave it away. Iwan looked just like Ifor and I blurted out his name. Lowri covered real quick and I've never given it any thought since…'

'You're not responsible, Dewi,' Gethin objected and

around the table everyone joined in agreement.

'So this Phillips is on the war-path and someone here is helping him? And the reason Claudia and Seb aren't here today is that you and … Isabelle?… from Myrddin's Mutineers have figured out it's one of them?' Geraint asked.

Luke nodded at his father-in-law.

'What I'm finding it even harder to take in is why Alys and Emrys aren't here,' Dewi added, and assent echoed around the table.

'Like I said, I had a visit from Aislinn. She was supposed to have gone to Gerhard's funeral to be with Emrys, but she came to me to tell me that it was Claudia who'd caused Alys to miscarry and that made us wonder if it could be Claudia who's acting with Phillips. Until then, the only person me and Isabelle could imagine the traitor to be was Seb. He's the right age to be Iwan's son and we don't know anything about his background. So we needed to meet without Claudia or Seb because we didn't know who might be…' Luke ran a hand through his hair and grimaced. 'But there was something wrong about Aislinn not going to the funeral. I talked to Isabelle about it later that day. At first I was going to keep it a secret, like Aislinn asked me to, but it didn't make sense that someone that powerful would be afraid of Claudia and if she really did need help she'd need more than me. Isabelle contacted Morganne and apparently Aislinn had shown up for the funeral in Brittany, but…'

'People there saw her for who she really is.' Everyone around the table turned towards Alys, who stood at the top of the stairs in Capel Horeb. 'Of course Emrys realised too and he's broken by it. I've never seen him so defeated.'

'The people in Brittany, are they all like you and Emrys?' Gethin asked, breaking the silence.

'In what way?' Alys smiled and Luke realised he hadn't seen her smile in too long.

Gethin shrugged and held out his hands. 'I don't know quite how to put it. I've lived with it all my life, a sort of unspoken open secret. Growing up with Emrys and seeing what happened in the raids from E-Gov, meeting people like Gerhard. Then Vivian and Morganne. You're not…'

'We're completely human, Geth. If you poison us, do we not die? Or at least lose our babies?'

Gethin coloured. 'I wasn't saying you're…'

'I know. Sorry. But you're right. We are human, but not as… Let's just say we're a little more than. I don't mean better… but we carry other lives inside us… other personas, you might say.'

'And Aislinn—what did you mean when you said in Brittany they could see her for who she really is?'

'Aislinn is… something very different. She's not like me and Emrys. She's a baobhan sith.' Alys paused. The whole room seemed to be holding a single breath. 'She appears as a beautiful woman, always in that long green dress. Of course, there's no reason to suspect every beautiful woman who wears green and I don't imagine any of us asked to check that her feet weren't deer hooves, but in Brocéliande no one needed to ask questions. They could see through the illusion. She's a vampire of sorts. Normally they prey on hunters, but any powerful man who is lonely and wants a woman in his life will do. Sometimes they enchant their victims with a dance to exhaustion. Eventually, the talons are out and she slits open her victim to drain his blood.'

'I really can't take all this in,' Seren said quietly.

Owain stared at his sister. 'So you're telling us there are vampires as well as… as people who are more than people… It's like my life's getting rewritten backwards. All that code breaking you did… was any of it even maths or…'

'Maths and magic, Owain. Sometimes there's not a lot of difference between them.'

Owain looked from Alys to Luke. 'And you? Are you more than human, too?' His voice was a little louder than needed.

Luke shook his head. 'No.'

'But he is Artu. He is the one who returns with the light whenever people stand their ground.'

'I'm not sure about that,' Luke said. 'There's nothing special about me…'

'And Myrddin Emrys… hiding in plain sight, I presume?' Geraint asked.

'Yes,' Alys agreed. 'He's never hidden his name here, though he's someone who has had other personas, sometimes more than one at once. You all knew he was Luke's dad and also known as Nazir Malik.'

'Everyone just accepted that Emrys disappeared sometimes, away doing trade or obscure stuff with computers. So it didn't seem that weird that he'd had another life over the border,' Seren said.

Zach stood up. 'This is a lot to take in for all of us—betrayal, vampires, humans who happen to be… more—but I think you're telling us that the only person accusing Claudia of anything was this fake Aislinn, which means the thing we're here to discuss just got a whole lot clearer.'

'Thank you, Zach,' Dewi said. 'He's right, isn't he, Alys?'

'Yes. Claudia is as loyal as me, as any of us in this room. But Seb…'

'What do we do?' Cei spoke up.

'Keep him off our scent,' Kyle put in. 'Give him projects that seem really important for him to leak to

Phillips. Keep him busy. Have dummy meetings of the Gader just to stop him suspecting anything. We can feed him a lot of misinformation that way while we gather ourselves.'

Luke grinned across at Kyle. 'Brilliant,' he said.

'Absolutely ace, mate,' Zach agreed.

'Is there a real Aislinn?' Luke asked.

'Yes. She's very sick, but now the baobhan sith's been revealed she's back home and in good hands.'

'So we go to work.' Moriaen had sat, listening and pensive, but he stood and gently lifted the now sleeping Gwion from Saskia, who was still pacing with the baby. 'We go to work for him and all the ones coming after him in a place that still values freedom and community. We go to work in whatever ways we can—Emrys and Alys have the maths and magic, the rest of us have plenty of skills. Most of all, we believe in this place.'

As the chorus of assent finally subsided, Moriaen handed the still sleeping Gwion back to his mother.

'Thank you,' Seren said, 'I needed some cheer today.'

'We all did,' Dewi agreed. 'So we're pretty sure who our traitor is. All we need now is a plan for putting Kyle's idea of misinformation into action on the one hand, and a real stream of maths and magic aimed at taking down Phillips on the other.'

'A two-pronged approach, yes.'

‘Emrys!’ Alys ran to him and hugged him.

‘I owe you all an apology,’ Emrys began. He looked as though he had aged a decade in the last few days.

‘No,’ Alys said. ‘You were under an enchantment. Nearly everyone in this room was under her spell to some degree and so were Eoganan and Carvorst. We have good allies there so I think we should actually plan for three-prongs. I know we want to focus on our own security, but our allies need help with their strategy with the EEC. If we thought it was hard to secure autonomy here, it’s got even harder now. Dewi, Owain, Dad, this is your area.’ She turned to Emrys. ‘Can you ask Morganne to send Laurent and Elaine to help? We could do with a couple of people who can create a virtual environment for meetings that isn’t actually on any net or Connexion.’

Emrys nodded. ‘Good, yes. That leaves the two of us free to stay focussed here—one for diverting Seb, the other for the real sabotage.’

‘Maybe the Mutineers could loan us Isabelle too,’ Luke suggested. ‘We need to not fail this time.’

‘I’ll see if her brother will make the trip as well. Louis and Isabelle can keep track of Seb…’

‘Do you think he’s connected?’ Moriaen put in.

Emrys whistled. ‘Of course! Of course he’ll be connected. Latest model no doubt. Damn! We could have been jamming that for years if only we’d…’

'No second guessing,' Alys cut in. 'If Isabelle and Louis concentrate on jamming the tag he's probably not going to be up to much film-making or anything else. He'll get disoriented, have headaches, massive brain fog.'

'All the stuff he pretended to have when he arrived here,' Zach added. 'And I know you said no second guessing, but I feel pretty bad about being the one who suggested he make films for us.'

'We do the good we can with the knowledge we have,' Moriaen said.

Zach shrugged. 'You're right, mate.'

'Okay, so this is a possible plan,' Emrys said. 'Me and Luke head back across the border. I'll set Luke up as a lobbyist for a Saudi Arabian company wanting in on nanotechnology and offering some impressive leaps forward that neither Hunter's nor Hengst Futures can deliver yet. The aim is to get as much information as possible on Phillips's insider relationships with these civil servants and ministers. See what they'll let slip when they're shown enough money and given enough alcohol. We want a scandal so big that the guy's stocks crash overnight at the very least.

'I'm going to be pretty intrusive, Luke. I'll need to see everything you see and feed it back to Alys to capture here. Then Moriaen and Zach can take what I send and do some of our own film-making.'

'Kyle and Gethin,' Moriaen said. 'I've got another idea for me and Zach. You said this waitress who talked to you, who you'd known at school, told you her mum's name and that Ross bought her as a baby after getting the mum pregnant. Then he dumped the girl when she wasn't useful, right? So how about we find the mum? The girl too. They both might like to see Hengst with no future. Me and Zach can go to the Subs, do some digging.'

Luke shot Emrys a beseeching look. His father knew the whole story, but the Gader didn't.

'Hm, nice idea, but maybe just the mother. We suspect Katie may be playing both sides. Something she let slip to Isabelle. We might be wrong but if we can find my apparent half-sister, she seems to be the one who lost everything after starting out with very little in the first place.'

'Okay,' Moriaen agreed. 'Mission to find Jasmine Malik it is. You up for it?'

'Absolutely, mate,' Zach said, 'As long as you're okay with that, babe?'

'Stay safe,' Saskia said. 'But yes, I'll be fine.'

Seren looked from Saskia to Zach. 'Are you… Sorry, I'm being nosey now…'

'Yes, yes we're having a baby. We weren't going to say anything for a bit. Not with… with everything Alys was going through and it's only early, but…'

Alys walked over to Saskia and hugged her. 'That's wonderful news.' She turned to Zach. 'I'm thrilled for you both.'

Zach joined them in the group hug.

'So, let's recap,' Emrys said, 'If this is in order, Dewi?'

'So far it all sounds amazing,' Dewi agreed. 'Out of this world, to be fair, but I'm trying to get my mind round that.'

'Thank you. So we ask the Mutineers to send us four people. Laurent and Elaine to help our allies in the Highlands. Isabelle and Louis to keep Seb off his game or keep him busy with dummy projects if he can manage the energy to do anything. Meanwhile, I'll provide Luke with a complete alter-persona, not just a name change—you'll look completely different. This time they are not going to see us coming. The aim is to get really major information on Hengst's political string-pulling. We want maximum exposure on the financial corruption. Alys will get full visuals as well as audio and Geth and Kyle will work with her to convert it to video and plant it on as many sites as possible. To add impact, Moriaen and Zach will search for Jasmine Malik and interview her. If we find her, we should get her to somewhere safe too.'

'Our friends in the Highlands?' Geraint suggested. 'I'm figuring a half sister with a lot of issues might not be comfortable on your doorstep, Emrys?'

'For both of us, probably. Yes, I can arrange that.' Around the room there were nods and murmurs of assent. 'Good. So, operation Badon Hill it is.' He put a hand on Luke's shoulder and looked into his eyes. 'This will be your victory, Artu.'

February 28, 2083

Two senior ministers of U-Gov resigned today amidst allegations that they had accepted substantial payments as well as other benefits in return for expediting licences to test the eagerly-awaited new generation nano-connector, Linkit, on human volunteers, despite evidence of serious side effects in an early and highly controversial trial.

Henry Simpson, Minister for Well-being, and Lucinda Barker-Cullen, Minister for Technology, issued a joint statement denying any breaches of protocol or wrong doing. The ministers have said that their resignations were made to protect U-Gov from the smear campaign against them.

Ms Barker-Cullens's portfolio will be taken over by rising star of U-Gov, Cerdic (Dick) Phillips, son of Ross Phillips. This surprising and potentially contentious appointment is being seen as a clear signal that U-Gov intends to work closely and transparently with the tech giants, both Hengst Futures, founded and run by Phillips' father, and rival tech giant, Hunter's. Mr Phillips Jr. promised an impartial and streamlined route to licensing that ensures maximum safety and privacy whilst allowing both companies to enhance the lives of citizens.

'The old abuses of E-Gov bear no relation to U-Gov's forward-thinking and life-optimising policies,' Mr Phillips claimed. 'We are fortunate to have in our small country two international leaders in safe, healthy Connexions, each with a particular constituency that makes them complimentary assets to our nation's ability to dominate a global market.'

Mr Phillips Jr. refused to comment on the current allegations surrounding his father, which have led to rapidly falling stock value for Hengst Futures. Accusations include not only high-level bribes, but also abusive employment practices and a sexually charged and intimidating environment at the company's glamorous labs in central Birmingham. Further rumours that Ross Phillips bought his own daughter from her drug-addicted mother, who was then living in the Telford Subs, and that his aim was to groom his daughter to infiltrate the rival Hunter empire, have also been denied by the family.

March 15, 2083

After almost three weeks of revelations of sexual, employment and financial abuses, founding tech-tycoon of Hengst Futures, Ross Phillips, was today found dead in his luxury apartment located in Hengst Grand Central, the flagship laboratory and tech-complex of the company that has been dogged by recent allegations. It is believed that Mr Phillips had taken his own life.

Ross Phillips is survived by his son, the Minister of Technology, Cerdic (Dick) Phillips and a daughter, Katie, who it is rumoured Phillips bought as a baby with the intention of using her as sexual bait. The daughter's whereabouts remain unknown. He also has an uncle, Iwan Jones, formerly known as Iwan Tigaen, who owns a major stake in Hengst Futures, and a cousin, Sebastian Jones, who is believed to have fled to the neighbouring country of Y Tir after the demise of E-Gov in 2075.

Iris: falling through myth 3

Shine, Shapash, shine!
You are the torch,
the lamp of the gods, the sun.
You are Shapash, burning radiance…

I fall into your light,
I am Iris supplanted by Hermes.
I am Ninšubur, dulled out of sight by Papsukkal
I am Shapash, goddess of the sun, messenger to the high god, my father, Ēl.

Offerings were made to me, as to my brother, Baal, my sister, Anat.

I was the lamp of the gods, the oracle of mortals, their protector from serpents.

I was the mother of the stallion and the mare, bestowing my blessings from the twin peaks of Sapan.

In Ugarit and across Phoenicia my name was loved.

I was the bridge between worlds.

It was me who carried Baal's body back to Mount Sapan and, when he returned to life, me who intervened in his battle against Mot, saving his life so he would become monarch among gods.

I was the lamp of the gods, but new people came.

My name was forbidden, my light dimmed.

There was one who shone with my light, whose name was my name in his tongue.

He was a hero, the carrier of my light, the remnant of my name.

Samson was granted extraordinary strength by his god. He wrestled with a lion, killed an army with only the jawbone of an ass. But his strength was taken. He ended his days, this great deliverer, eyeless in Gaza at the mill with slaves, but at the last his strength returned, enough for him to tear down a temple with his hands, killing his Philistine captors and himself, killing my light for ever. The price of victory is self-destruction, after all.

Shine, Shapash, shine!
You are the torch,
the lamp of the gods, the sun.
You are Shapash, burning radiance…

I am gone. I will not return.
I am Iris.
I am Ninšubur.
I am Shapash.

I am supplanted and my light extinguished.

I am falling…
fallling through myth…

7

November 1 2083

In the upstairs mezzanine of Capel Horeb, Claudia and Kyle were busy laying the long table while Osian and Saskia, baby Jonah sleeping in the sling hugging her body, offered each other tastes of their dishes.

'Delicious,' Osian said. 'You sure mine's not too salty?'

'It's perfect.' Saskia reassured. 'We just need Alys and Gwen's salads and Zach and Moriaen's cakes and we'll have a feast.'

'Certainly smells amazing,' a voice said, as Laurent appeared at the top of the stairs, carrying a tray of cakes.

'It does that, babe,' Zach said from behind Laurent, appearing with more cakes.

'Aw, didn't know you felt that way, babe,' Osian quipped, winking at Zach.

'Hey, get your own, Osh.' Saskia nudged Osian playfully and waited for Zach to put his tray on the table before throwing her arms around him. 'All mine,' she said with a grin.

Zach stroked Jonah's soft hair, protruding from the sling. 'How's he been, babe?'

'A dream. Fed madly then zonked out so I could cook.'

The room began to fill. Alys and Gwen set salads along the table and Gethin arrived with drinks.

'Emrys, Luke and Dewi will be along with Eoganan and Carvorst soon,' Elaine announced as she entered the room.

Alys watched the way she always addressed Laurent even when talking to a group. But Laurent seemed always unaware. He caught Alys's eye and smiled, coming towards her.

'I could finish putting the salads out for you,' he offered, 'or get you a drink.'

Alys shook her head. 'Thanks, I'm fine. How about you, Elaine? Your husband's offering to be the waiter for the evening.'

Elaine coloured slightly. 'Apple juice would be great,' she said.

'Right, yes, er…'

'I can get it myself,' Elaine offered.

'Sorry, no, I was… let me get it for you.'

'How did it go with Seb?' Alys asked Elaine.

'I wasn't in the meeting, but Isabelle and Louis said he didn't put up any resistance.'

Gwen came and stood with the group as Laurent returned with Elaine's juice. 'It feels so strange,' Gwen said. 'We've had people betray us before—our own people, but Ifor was allowed to leave and I suppose poor

Sion would have been too if he'd lived. I don't think we've ever had someone we're effectively imprisoning.'

Alys patted her mum's arm. 'I know. I think everyone feels weird about it. I'm glad Seb's family left and went back to U-Gov when they couldn't take the life here. I don't know how we'd handle keeping a whole family under house arrest.'

More gathered around the conversation. 'Maybe they never were his family,' Gethin suggested. 'Knowing what we know now, maybe they were people he hired to make his cover story really good. And then we all felt so sorry for him when they ran off.'

'That makes such sense, mate,' Zach put in. 'Right from the start he had us in there helping and getting real friendly. We wouldn't have made his plumbing such a priority if it'd been a single guy, even if we sympathised. The film-making, the so-called friends who knew stuff about the new tags, the family in need of help — he had it all going on.'

'Well now he's got worse that nothing,' Gwen said, 'And I'm the one who'll take the tag out of him to cut his ties to what he might have had.'

'And if we didn't take his tag and keep him safely here, he'd bring hell down on us without a second thought,' Geraint said, putting his arm round Gwen's shoulder. 'I know it's harsh, cariad, but he hasn't thought twice about what he's been doing for the last eight years. It's not as though we're torturing or killing him…'

Gwen smiled weakly. 'I know. And I know we're doing the right thing, but in a way it is torture. These people with their tags and all that gives them—they become… I don't want to say they're not human, and I'm not going to dignify all the twaddle about how they're "enhanced" and "improved", but they are definitely changed by it. And more and more of the world is going the same route. It's exhausting just thinking about what the world is going to be like for anyone who insists on remaining "merely human". Some days it feels like we're the mad ones.'

'But we're not, Mam,' Alys said quietly. 'And we're not the only resistance. We're celebrating Scotland getting recognised as a sovereign state tonight and then there's Brittany and the Caribbean islands.'

'And an enclave in Greece,' Laurent put in. 'My mum's asked me to visit them after we leave here. The New Olympians.'

'My sister always loved Greek mythology—all that shape-shifting. Is this new community gifted?' Emrys asked.

He was standing with Luke, Eoganan and Carvorst. Alys couldn't help remembering the last time she'd been in this room with these same people.

'Mum says they're not, or at least she thinks the

community's so traumatised that even their mages have forgotten their powers. Greece has had a century of hell—wildfires, temperature rises and the deaths that go with it, loss of coastline and complete economic collapse. These folks seem to have just sat it out. Now there are plans to use the Greek population to experiment on…'

'Surely you mean they're being given the opportunity to "volunteer" to be the first to receive life-enhancing technology that will pave the way for the rejuvenation of the Greek economy?' Kyle offered.

'Yeah, that's exactly how it'll be sold to them,' Zach agreed. 'And this group of New Olympians see through all the lies. Good for them.'

'It's going to be hard for them without any extra resources,' Elaine said.

'Completely agree,' Carvorst said, 'It's been almost impossible for us. We only have me and Aislinn and she's been out of action for a while, though improving rapidly now. This last year, with her sick, I couldn't have maintained our meta-saces for hidden meetings on my own. It takes the likes of Emrys or Alys to wield that much power. It made all the difference having Laurent and Elaine to help. The New Olympians have a hard road ahead.'

'So should I come and help too?' Elaine turned towards Laurent. Alys saw the flicker of dismissal cross his face and hoped Elaine hadn't noticed it.

'Maybe next visit, love. This is just a discovery mission at the moment. Best I go alone. Though it's a shame you can't spare Alys, Luke. Think these people could do with someone really powerful and with the maths to match it.'

Luke shot Alys a look that she didn't return. 'If Alys thought she should be going with you, she'd make her own decision, Laurent. We might be channelling some deep myth in The Standing Ground, but we don't have dark age views on men giving their wives permission to go places.'

Laurent laughed uncomfortably and three other people began new lines of conversation, including Isabelle, who pulled Luke aside.

'Does Alys know about Katie?' she whispered.

'Enough. She knows… she knows I ran into a girl I liked at school and that… something happened.'

'You mean she doesn't know that it was *the* Katie Lomax, who caused you all that trouble at school, then turned out to Ross Phillips's daughter and probably a plant all along? The same Katie Lomax whose father, whatever she felt about him, committed suicide after we exposed his corruption?'

Luke nodded.

'And Emrys has allowed this?'

'He's not happy. But he says it will be worse if it comes

from him and I should tell her everything myself.'

Isabelle's eyes widened. 'And you're going to do that when?'

'She's had such an awful year already, I…'

'Artu, in your name…'

Isabelle lifted a warning finger and shook her head as Luke began to protest that he might not be Artu…

'In *your name* we won a great battle. I know there's more to come. We're watching Hengst regroup and Hunter's are still thriving. We all know we're heading deeper into the darkness, Luke. You need to face this and tell Alys before you leave for U-Gov again.'

'You're heading back to U-Gov?' Alys asked, joining them.

Luke gulped, wondering how much of the conversation she had heard.

'Dick Phillips is getting more powerful,' Luke said.

'Yes,' Alys agreed. 'We think he'll make a play for the Prime Minister's position soon and there'll be no more pretence of U-Gov if he gets in. He wants the old regime back. Connect or be on the margins. He's already talking about how life should be made unbearable for anyone who doesn't "voluntarily" opt in to the next generation of enhancements. He doesn't care whether it's with Hengst or Hunter's either. Hengst's tech division's is desperately trying to rally. Iwan Tigaen thinks he can out-compete

Hunter's by promising a new generation of enhancements with so called privacy controls. No mention of keeping the government out, of course. But the truth is, operation Badon Hill did real damage to Hengst. At the moment, they're only a small thorn in the world's side compared to Hunter's, no matter how they posture.'

'And Hengst already pulled in a lot less money before our work, didn't they?' Isabelle asked.

'Much less. Hengst might entice some of the rich to invest in their enhancements because they're stupid enough to think they can shut out the corporates and go back to some kind of halcyon E-Gov-era with old-style population control. But E-Gov was a blip in the history of power. These big corporations make all governments look like children playing house.' Alys turned towards Luke. 'If you're leaving Y Tir again, you should be focusing on Hunter's. They're the big threat to all of us and they've started to use Hengst's ploy of offering "free" goodies to the unwary and desperate in addition to their premium tiers. Moriaen's done amazing work tracking what's going on there, but it's time we stopped them.'

Alys turned and walked back to the table as Dewi began calling everyone to take a seat.

'She might not know everything, but your wife knows you are lying to her, Luke. Don't go into the dark with this left raw between you.'

Alys watched Isabelle walk away from Luke to find herself a seat at the far end of the table. She watched Luke hesitate as though he was lost before he went to sit near Eoganan, leaving a seat free next to her for Laurent to slip into.

'Why so sad, beautiful Alys? Let me pour you a drink.'

Iris: in the body of the plant

Once my rainbow connected the gods to their worshippers on earth. And the caduceus was mine.

I did not know where these words came from or what kind of being might utter them. I knew nothing of gods. There was only this body on the burnt-out earth. I felt the scorching heat, sensed the sun's light, but could see nothing for I had neither shoots nor leaves to watch and follow the sun. I was parched, my onion-paper skin drying in the desiccating heat. The scent of burnt-out fires permeated me and the wind brought only the rank breath of devastation, scalding in gusts.

It went on like this, day after searing day. I would shrivel here, be cremated by sun and wind, become part of the parched dust of this land. My suffering would end in death.

I tried to remember.

Rainbows spilled from my coat, rain poured from the clouds I seeded with ocean storms.

There was no meaning in the sounds, only an aching babble.

I did not remember.
There was nothing.
Soon I would return to the earth.

A vibration juddered through the dried-out husk of me.

There was sound.
A voice.
The wind shifting.

Then silence.
A shadow.

A shadow stooped to the dry surface.
For a moment, I was shaded from the blaze of the sun.

And I felt…

There was a softness in the touch, even a hint of moisture.

I was lifted, then felt myself drop.
Not onto the earth again.

Into darkness, the vibrations pulsing through me, a drum beat against the earth as I moved within this dark space, not cool, but sheltered.

I was Iris, goddess of rainbows, carrier of words.

The meaningless syllables shuddered through me.
I was resigned to whatever came next.
I did not remember.

8

Sunday 10 December, 2084, St Deiniol Gwyn's Day

Alys shivered and pulled the covers closer, peering at the clock. 9 a.m. She still felt the urge to hunker down and hibernate. She'd felt it since the pregnancy but it had deepened after losing Brân, persisted even through the spring and summer and now she was facing a winter alone. She got out of bed and shook herself. She could hear Luke in Bwthyn Heddychlon's kitchen and hoped he was making porridge.

'Good timing,' he said as she came into the kitchen. 'Busy day.'

'I wish you were going to be here for the Solstice. It's going to be hard for Claudia too.'

'I know.' He didn't make eye contact.

They had become less awkward with each other over the year, but they had not re-found the ease that had existed before Brân, or before Luke went to Birmingham and… Alys shook herself again.

'You okay?'

'Sorry, yes. Porridge smells good.' She busied herself putting honey and seeds on the table to add to their bowls. Luke had already made a pot of coffee. A treat day.

'It'll already be a hive of activity at Ty Meirion,' Luke said, bringing over the steaming bowls of porridge.

'Mam's really nervous about officiating as well.'

Luke laughed. 'She's got Morganne to help her. Nothing could possibly be allowed to go wrong.'

'Emrys will miss Gerhard being there.'

Luke nodded. 'It's a big loss, isn't it? Weird, I hardly knew my grandfather till the last few years, but when I met him it was like I remembered him from when I was really young, from when my mum…'

'I miss my taid every day. Tomas would've loved this. I didn't know my other taid. He died in the first pandemic, or Nain Megan, Dad's mam. But I'm glad Nain Anwen will be there. I think she'll live a long life like Nain Parry. It feels good having all these generations…'

Alys hesitated and Luke put a hand on her arm. 'They'll be there in spirit—Gerhard and my mum, Tomas and Megan and your other taid—all the ancestors and all the… Innogen—both Innogens—the baby Gerhard and Lydie lost and the one who died with my mum—Vivian was going to name her after the sister she'd never known.' Luke's voice choked a little and he held onto Alys's arm more tightly. 'And Brân too. They'll all be there.'

Alys smiled and cupped her hand over Luke's, squeezing it.

'Yes, I think you're right. They will. But we'd better get

into gear and go and help this wedding to happen. I don't think anyone ever thought Emrys would marry, but I'm glad it's Claudia.'

'Me too. When I was young I used to look for signs to see if some woman had been in Nazir's house—ha! I still think of him as Nazir sometimes. He must have noticed what I was doing. I sometimes wonder if it was me that stopped him finding anyone. Ironic, my pod mother is becoming my step-mother, but wonderful too.'

'Not much honeymoon though,' Alys said, putting the porridge bowls into the sink and running water into them.

'Two days—no, not much, but we really need to be in place before Winterval starts in Birmingham. There'll be a lot of office parties with the guards down. Weird how those who are making tags so that people can live virtually continue to have so many in-person events.'

'You're not staying in the Centre?'

'No, Hunter's have taken over a building in Cannon Hill Park up near Edgbaston—used to be an arts centre. Think they've extended it quite a bit too. We're in a revived hotel that opened up again to serve Hunter's clientele or staff from other places. It's exotic to travel rather than mind link, apparently. Edgbaston Park Hotel. Emrys has hired an apartment in it so we can have meetings and avoid restaurants. And I've got a swanky deluxe room with real plumbing.'

Alys swatted him playfully. 'We have plumbing here.'

'Yeah,' he grinned, 'but not like this, with all the tech controls and endless hot water.'

'Well don't fall so in love with the plumbing that you over-stay.'

'It'll be strange being away for Solstice.'

'It will. But Emrys wouldn't set it up like this if it wasn't what's needed. I'm more than aware how urgent it is to take Hunter's down. Moriaen says they are getting so many of Hengst's former subscribers on their new Transense-Lite that they can hardly keep up with the sign-ups and amount of new tags they're fitting.'

Luke nodded. 'Yeah, doesn't seem to matter how cheesy the slogans get. People just keep signing up—*With neurolife-lite you get a free life for free. Now that's Transense.*'

'Can't believe anyone would go for that.' Alys paused. 'So yes, I know you and Emrys need to do this, but just promise me…'

Luke gulped. 'You don't need to worry, I…'

Alys kissed his cheek. 'I know. Now let's move. I'm looking forward to seeing Morganne and…'

'Laurent?'

'I was going to say Galaad, actually. Elaine is loving being a mother. And Morganne is apparently the doting grandmother.'

Alys woke from a strange dream, a drum still beating as she came round. She opened her eyes. The same drumming. Da-da-da-dah—da da da dah… The door, someone was at the door, the knocking becoming louder, more urgent.

She pulled a jumper over her nightdress and fumbled to find leggings in a pile beside the bed.

'Coming—I'm coming.'

'Alys?'

At the door was a woman her own age, pale oval face and straight brown hair. She looked dishevelled and her eyes were rimmed red. On her hip was a toddler, a little boy of about one.

'Yes, I'm Alys, I…'

'Can I come in? It's important—please.'

'Alys opened the door wider and stepped out of the way.

'I'm Katie,' the woman said as she walked past her. 'Katie Lomax. And this is Maurice. He's…'

'Luke's,' Alys said. She heard her own voice, far away and flat and felt her temperature drop.

Katie put the toddler down and turned to face Alys.

'Maybe in the kitchen,' Alys said, trying to keep her voice steady. She pointed at the door to the left and Katie went in, the child following her.

Alys gestured to the table and filled a kettle before

sitting opposite Katie.

'He told you?'

'He told me something happened in Birmingham with someone he'd known at school. You're the girl who got him into the fight with Bradley Hunter and started the whole chain of events that made him come searching for Y Tir, aren't you?'

'Ha! I didn't know I'd been that effective. Yeah. He had a thing for me in school.'

'You told him you didn't go out with "darkie Messers" if I remember what he told me. The fight nearly got him sent to that torture camp where they "re-formed" people.'

'I had a script to follow. Well, not word for word, but my dad bought me from my no-good darkie mum so I could grow up to seduce Bradley Hunter. Luke was getting in the way. I didn't realise then we were related of course. Stupid really. My mam had the same surname but I just thought it must be common name amongst those people.'

'Those people?'

'Arabs, blacks, whatever they are. I was lucky it didn't show in me. If I hadn't looked white I suppose my dad would've left me with my druggie mum. Anyway, Luke wasn't my type and he definitely wasn't who Dad wanted me to target.'

Alys breathed deeply and hoped her disgust wasn't

showing too clearly. The kettle began to whistle and she stood up.

'Would your little boy like anything? I've got some apple juice I could water down or some fruit and oat cakes?'

'Yes, please.'

'Quiet! What did I tell you?'

Alys turned. 'You're welcome,' she addressed Maurice. Juice or fruit or both?'

'Both please.'

'Maurice!'

'Your son's very clever,'

'My son's a freak. That's why I've brought him here. He's a freak and I'm no use to Uncle Iwan while I'm saddled with him. I want you to take him. He's Luke's. If you don't take him, I'll dump him somewhere, put him in a home or take him to my mother in the Subs.'

'You'll find Jasmine's moved on,' Alys said quietly. 'But yes, I'll take him.' Alys felt shock pulsing through her, but there was no hesitation. 'Maurice, how would you like to stay with me for a while? Me and your daddy? He's… he's out just now, but he'll love you to stay with us too. What do you think?'

Maurice glanced at Katie, who nodded.

'I'd like to stay here,' he said. 'Do you have toys?'

Alys laughed, the relief of such a normal wish from the

precocious toddler.

'Well, I don't yet, but we'll get some. You'll have loads of uncles who'll make some for you—Owain and Gethin and Osian. And children to play with too—Gwion's a bit older than you and Jonah's about your age, though…'

'It's alright if they can't talk. I'm weird.'

'Oh, darling, no, you're…'

'Special? Why don't you tell him he's "special"? It's just freak by another name. Are you pouring that tea any time soon?'

Alys bit her tongue and poured herb tea that Katie sniffed at suspiciously while Maurice devoured a plate of apple slices, blueberries and oat cakes.

'Your granddad could talk like you when he was a little boy,' Alys told him as he ate. 'He came to Tanygrisiau when he was very little too. Some people thought he was odd, but all the people who mattered loved him.'

When Katie had left, Alys bundled Maurice into his thin coat. There was a small bag of clothes left in the hallway for him, no doubt fabrics that wouldn't like to be washed. She would ask Seren for some of Gwion's grown-out-of things, though only to borrow. Seren and Owain would need them back for the next baby.

'Hello! Anyone here?'

Alys hoped her mother would be at home, but wished

Tomas was alive. Emrys's wedding a few days earlier and Luke leaving on his mission with Emrys had made her think about Tomas even more than usual. She heard Gwen's tread on the stairs, coming down to the kitchen.

'Hello, cariad, and who's this lovely little person?'

'I'm Maurice Malik,' he answered for himself.

Alys watched Gwen blink and look confused.

'Maurice, this is my mam. She'll be your nain, your grandmother, and I bet she's got some toys tucked away if we ask her nicely.'

They settled the child with a wooden train set that had been Owain's and recently fetched out of the loft ready to go to him and Seren for Gwion.

Gwen set a pot of coffee on the table and chocolate brownies. 'Think we might need the big guns,' she said. 'Milk or water for Maurice?'

Maurice looked up from fitting tracks together. 'I'm fine thank you, Nain.'

'Right. Well, just give us a shout if you need anything.'

He nodded and went back to the serious business of fitting carriages to engines.

'Okay, I think I'm ready. I assume Luke is his dad?'

Alys nodded. 'He looks so like him, doesn't he? Do you think everyone will realise?'

'People here are good at not seeing what others don't

want them to. Think of all that Tomas saw and kept to himself. And some people won't want to see, which is a skill of its own. I'm hoping your dad will be one of those.'

'And Owain.'

'Quite.' Gwen lifted a large brownie onto her plate. 'And Maurice's mum?'

'Katie Lomax.'

'Missing daughter of the late Ross Phillips?'

'The same.'

'Did you know?'

'Some of it. Not that there was a child.'

Gwen lowered her voice to a whisper. 'And she doesn't…'

'Mummy doesn't want me, no,' Maurice offered, without breaking the progress of his trains.

'Right. You must feel sad about that…'

'A bit. But I think I'll like it here better.'

'Good. And how would you like to stay with me for a bit. I mean if Alys…'

Alys shook her head. 'No. Maurice should live with us. But we'll need something to tell Dad and Owain. Even if they know we're making it up… or suspect. Something that they can tell themselves.'

Gwen put her hands over both of Alys's and held them tight. 'You've had a hard year, cariad.'

'I feel like I've been in a long hibernation and I think

I was about to go deeper in this winter with Luke away. Maybe this'll bring me back to myself. We'll spend Alban Arthan with you?'

'Of course you will. I wouldn't let you be alone at Solstice even if I had to break your door down. I've invited Claudia too. And Gethin and Osh. They're both motherless and Osh is a good cook.'

'How about Kyle and Moriaen?'

'Cei's got them an invite to Dewi and Lowri's, along with Zach and Saskia and the babe. Or maybe it was Leuci that got Cei to invite Moriaen with Kyle as the cover story.'

Alys laughed. 'Subtle. It would be good to see those two together.'

'We thought we'd all get together the day after—pool the leftovers down at Capel Horeb.'

'Sounds good. And gives me time to get some Solstice presents organised for little man here.'

'A train would be good,' Maurice put in. 'But I know this one's Gwion's.'

'There's an unseemly amount of it, cariad. I'll have a word with Owain and see how we can divvy it up.'

Maurice grinned. 'Am I allowed chocolate?'

Gwen laughed. 'We don't often have it. Bit of a precious commodity here. But today you certainly are allowed. I mean if…'

Alys nodded. 'What would you like to call me, Maurice?' she asked.

He pursed his lips, thinking. 'Mam, like the way you say it here. Not 'mummy', though.'

'Mam it is.'

March 18, 2084

Alys sighed and pushed away the remains of her tea. She was glad Owain and Seren had arrived to take Maurice walking with them and Gwion. He would be away for his first overnight stay, which made her anxious, but she wouldn't want him picking up on her unannounced guest's intentions.

'I thought I'd stay for Alban Eilir,' Laurent said. I've brought you something from Greece.

'You shouldn't have. And you should be home with Elaine for Alban Eilir.'

'Elaine's got the baby and my mother's all over both of them, they're fine.'

'It's lucky Elaine's got Morganne with you away so long. It's been over a year. Elaine must miss you.'

'I went back for the birth…'

'Briefly,' Alys put in. 'And are you finished in Thessaly now?'

'They're as ready as they're ever going to be to apply for

independent stateship. Y Tir started a trend—the Scots and now the New Olympians. It's a hard place to live. Its economy has been in terminal decline all century—pandemic, wild fires, then coastal flooding. But they're a determined lot. I think they'll pull it off, but I was really hoping to talk…'

'No.'

'You're reading my mind now?'

'I don't have to. I'm married to Luke.'

'And how's that working out for you?'

'What? I don't know what…'

'Alys. I don't know what the thing is between the two of you. But last I saw, it didn't look good. And me and Elaine… I don't know what to say… her dad pretty much pushed her on me and she was beautiful and keen, but… there's no spark, Alys. And honestly, I don't think she'd have noticed if I hadn't turned up when Galaad was born. She was so wrapped up in him…'

'Don't be so absurd. She'd just given birth. You should both have been wrapped up in him. And whatever the future is for you and Elaine, I'm not part of it. I'm with Luke.'

'Who's where, by the way?'

'Away. Doing important work with Emrys. And back soon. Very soon.'

Laurent sighed and held up his hands in surrender.

'Shame, but if you ever change your mind...'

'I won't.'

'Fair enough. Anyway, like I said, I have something for you.'

'I don't...'

'Don't worry, it's not some extravagant love token, my lady Eluned. Silly really, I picked it up on the plain beneath Mount Olympus. The place used to have pine forest and shrubland, but it looks like a scorched moonscape now. It's as though the earth's rusted, a few black skeletons of trees. Really sad. And then there was this.'

He reached into his bag and handed her a single plant bulb.

Alys fingered the small bulb. It looked like a shallot onion, but longer and curling round itself at the tail. 'What is it?'

'An iris bulb. Very special plant in Greece. The New Olympians are taking its flower as their symbol. Just one iris bulb in a vast wasteland. Not sure why I thought of you when I saw it, but there you are... You can plant it, see if it blooms.'

'Maybe, or maybe I'll dry it and make tea,' Alys said. 'I've never had orris root tea, it's supposed to be pretty special.'

She rose and put the bulb on the windowsill, laying it

down gently. She felt a touch on her shoulder, but didn't move, entranced by the iris bulb. When she finally stirred Laurent had left. It had grown dark and the house was cold.

Iris: being born

Do you remember your passage from one world to another?

I remember little of how I came to be cocooned within this body, though there are images. Flashes of fire and unbearable pain. The melting of a rainbow and golden wings being ripped away. The overwhelming feeling of being desiccated by sun and wind. And a long journey, nothing but vibrations and darkness.

And I remember a soft warm hand cradling me. A voice I wanted to call out to: *mam mam*, the sound reflecting back to me, *fy mhlentyn, fy mhlentyn.*

I had come home, laid on a cool surface until I was lifted again.

The pain screamed through every atom of me. Cut and laid out, my body in slivers, drying, drying. Every fragment screaming: *mam, mam*, but there was no answering voice. There was only the certainty that I would finally die now, shredded and wizened.

I do not know how long I had floated here.

I had grown and ripened, my heart beating to the rhythm of another heart. The sounds of a body cloaking and comforting me. But today I was restless.

I felt my head pressing down, down. I wanted to keep pressing, pushing and as I pushed there was an opening, small, too small. But I pushed harder and harder. And my head entered a tunnel, moist and warm, its walls pressing against me, squeezing me. I pressed against the sides of this canal, dizzy and determined, obsessed with the need to push further.

I could not tell how long this went on. I knew that, for a while, dazed with the pressure, my pulse weakening, I slept. Perhaps more than once this happened. It was a blur and already I was forgetting.

And more than once, I thought the walls would cave in on me, that I'd be flattened, that I would never emerge. I felt my head, pressed, changing shape, the walls crushing me, tighter and tighter. And then there was air, its coolness on the top of my head and a feeling of pressure deep inside me. The urge to do something I had never done before. The urge to breathe. My body compressed as I emerged, gulping on air, exhausted and dazzled by the lights. The sounds and scents rushing into my body.

And amongst the sounds, was a voice I wanted to call out to: *mam mam*, the sound reflecting back to me, *fy mhlentyn, fy mhlentyn.*

'Iris,' the voice said. 'Welcome to the world, Iris

Anwen Vivian Selwyn-Malik.'

Iris.

There was something I had forgotten but it was no longer of any account. I had this life, and it would be everything.

I am Iris.

Iris Anwen Vivian Selwyn-Malik.

Part 2: If There's a Rainbow

9

June 2101

We moved to 2 Ty Meirion just after my second birthday. It had been abandoned before Nain was born and stood empty for decades but was slowly renovated after the people of Y Tir left their hide-out in the slate caverns in the 2040s. The old lady who lived there, Bethany, was 99 when she died, and her family were happy to pass on the house to us so that we would be next door to Taid and Nain and would have more space. Like Nain's house, the kitchen was on the ground floor with the living room and a bedroom on the middle floor and two more bedrooms and bathroom at the top. There was a small room behind the kitchen that Mam made into a study for her computers and we looked out over Taid's long garden that ran down half way down the street, following the line of the river.

I was not a precocious toddler like my brother, Maurice. Despite having a vivid memory of being in the womb, I came into this life forgetful, often feeling there was something important just out of mind. What I did possess from a young age was a profound sensitivity to the emotions of others, even before I could form the words for what I was experiencing. And I knew there was some great sadness between my parents.

They were together, though, in their constant defence of Y Tir. In the late 80s there were many political re-alignments across the European Community with more communities withdrawing from their national governments and being recognised as autonomous states, all of them resistant to the growing tide of mass-implants. Our Mutineer friends in Brittany also became an autonomous country, closely followed by the Basques and Catalonians, then the German-speaking Eupen-Malmedy province of Belgium, the Croats of Bosnia and Herzegovina, Moravians in the Czech Republic and the Faroese. There were more after them and in other regions around the world the same pattern was spreading.

Each time there were conflicts and each time the emerging state needed support. Our list of allies grew, but not our internal stability. My father had had his moment of glory when he'd invaded Hengst's empire with my grandfather's help, but their mission to sabotage Hunter's neurolife programme had not been a success. Somehow Hunter's always saw them coming and there was much soul-searching and suspicion that Y Tir must have another traitor, though none was ever found. On the worst occasion, my father was lucky to escape Hunter's Transense building alive and, triumphant, Hunter proceeded to drive home their advantage against the crumbling Hengst empire, leaving it a shadow of itself and no longer a competitor to their rising monopoly with its tentacles around the globe.

Moriaen worked tirelessly to find any chink in their armour, fuelled by his antipathy towards his racist father who had rejected him, but whenever he thought he was close, the chink would become an impenetrable wall. Sometimes we would make forays into E-Gov, as it had become again, dropping the pretence of the people's government that had been implied by "U-Gov". But my grandfather and mother needed most of their time to continually shore up the treaties that brought supplies into Y Tir. For all their maths and magic it was a struggle that sometimes failed and Nain would often say that things were as bad as the days after they emerged from the caverns, especially when medical supplies were scarce or interrupted entirely. Our allies in Occitania and Abkhazia helped to keep us fed, but other, older allies turned their backs, soured by the chain of new autonomous countries springing up around them or within their own borders and wanting no links with the tiny country that had begun this domino effect. To make things worse, the Hunter corporation added their own pressure, persuading or bribing the larger countries not to trade with what they described as "renegade nations".

We grew what food we could, had constant shortages, used electricity sparingly and vehicles hardly at all. But somewhere in the process of survival, I sensed that whatever sorrow had divided my parents had melted. They laughed together more and celebrated their fortieth birthdays with as much feasting as possible, aided by their circle of relations and friends who had been my extended family from birth.

Best of all, my Aunt Morganne stayed with us for the whole month that separated their birthdates.

'Sh, sh, just a nightmare, cariad. It's all gone away now.' Mam rocked me and my howls quelled to sobs and then sniffs. She wiped my face and nose again. 'All gone away,' she repeated. 'Do you want to sleep with us? Snuggle up with me and Dad?'

I shook my head and noticed someone in the doorway.

'She doesn't belong here,' my brother said. 'She's an alien. She's dreaming about where she's really from. The place where she betrayed her people and got thrown out.'

'Maurice! Of course Iris belongs here. She's my daughter, and your sister. You were there when she was born.'

'She's not my dad's daughter, though.'

'Maurice! That's a terrible thing to say. Go back to bed. We'll talk tomorrow.'

Maurice stared at me hard. 'You come from a bulb, not a father. You were dreaming of having your wings torn off, weren't you?'

I began to howl again and my Aunt Morganne arrived at the door. She put a hand on Maurice's head. 'Off to bed, young man. Don't worry, I'll take good care of your sister and mam.'

Maurice left but I kept wailing, rocked by Mam while Aunt Morganne stroked my back and sang a Breton lullaby. When I quieted again I asked to sleep with my aunty.

'Of course, sweetie.'

The next morning I stopped outside the kitchen door, hearing Mam and Aunt Morganne talking about me.

'The weird thing is that Laurent brought me an iris bulb from one of his trips to Greece. I dried it and made into tea and then I was pregnant. But surely she's still Luke's? I mean…'

'Of course she's Luke's. But she's also more than… She'll be a powerful young woman, Alys.'

'And Maurice knows?'

'Well, Maurice is darker than I was as a child, but he's definitely got insight.'

'Eavesdropping,' Maurice hissed behind me.

I startled and pushed open the kitchen door.

'Good morning, you two. I'm just doing porridge,'

Mam said, her cheer a little forced.

It had been Aunt Morganne who helped me remember myself. When I was seven she had taken me to Greece.

'So those mountains over there are…'

'Olympus,' I finished for her. 'And this is Petra.'

'You looked at a map?'

I shook my head. 'I just know.'

Morganne crouched down next to me. 'I think you are remembering, Iris. You know, your maman is… she's Alys and she's your mother, but she's also…'

'More than.'

'Yes. Me too and my brother, of course. You know the stories of Myrddin Emrys.'

I nodded. 'Maurice is more than too, isn't he? But not Dad, even though…'

'Even though he has a great destiny. Some of us are… we've been here before, not as mortals, Iris, but as people who lived longer ago than that, who returned and became part of human history. Human ourselves. And it doesn't always go exactly the same each time. Sometimes the Morganne I've been has been on a different side of the story. Sometimes I'm one aspect of Morganne and maybe someone else is another aspect of her. It's hard to explain. History both repeats and changes. We know we are here to be these roles, but the details shift each time.' Morganne hugged me to herself. 'Do you remember anything else?'

'I was the messenger of the gods,' I said. 'Then another one took my place and I think… I sort of woke up and knew they were horrible. I think I was horrible too, but I didn't want to be any more. I wanted them to change, but instead…'

She held me tight again. 'The things in your nightmares?'

I started to cry softly. 'Yes… yes… he…' I choked on the words.

'It's okay, sweetheart, you don't need to say anything.'

She held me while I sobbed and then held my hand as we walked back towards the village where we were staying.

'The place was different then,' I said quietly as we walked. 'It was so green and there were flowers everywhere.'

She squeezed my hand. 'It was a National Park even a hundred years ago. A World Biosphere Reserve. We've made a wasteland of so much of this world. Or drowned it as a result of our greed.'

'I think I was other messengers too, not just Iris. In other places. Maybe even at the same time. Could that be true?'

'Some of us "more thans" are archetypes, a few are more than that even.'

'Gods and goddesses. Will you teach me how to shape-shift like you taught Emrys?'

Morganne laughed. 'I will, though I think you'll be an easier student. Where will you begin?'

'With flight.'

'Of course.'

'Maurice is right, isn't he? I don't really belong in your story. I am an alien.'

'You do seem to have fallen through one myth only to land in another one,' she said, stopping and turning to face me. 'But you do belong. There's always a reason you land somewhere.'

Morganne

And so my darling niece remembered who she was. And I was thrilled to teach her, though always her learning was a rediscovery of what was already within. She was Iris, messenger of the gods, supplanted by Hermes. She was Ninšubur, vizier to Inanna and to An, messenger of the gods, and so much more. What she requested the gods gave. What she advised, the gods did. She was the mother of the land, a healer who was worshipped and fêted and yet she was eclipsed by the dullness of Papsukkal. She was Shapash, goddess of the sun, messenger to the high god, her father, Ēl, worshipped with her brother, Baal, her sister, Anat. She was the lamp of the gods, the oracle of mortals, their protector from serpents. But those who worshipped her were defeated by others. As fluid in gender as she was in changing shape, her light blazed in Samson, hero of his people, killed by his own hand. And still she was Iris, persisting down millennia, more than a story. So much power, more than any of us, and she carried it with grace and humility, falling out of her own myth and into ours to help the light to shine in the darkness. I was besotted with my grandchild, Galaad, a child who kept his innocence as he grew, and I taught him so much, but with this great-grand-niece, though I was seventy when we began to work together, I became young again, and felt my own power flexing for the battle that would surely come.

10

And so I began to learn why I'd arrived in another myth.

'A present for you,' Laurent announced, arriving at the lakeside where I was waiting for Aunt Morganne. He put a blade into my hands. A miniature side sword. 'Hold the hilt here behind the hand guard. Lovely. Nice weight, eh? It was made especially for you.'

I ran a finger down the blade and Laurent laughed.

'Not a real one?'

'It's real enough for practice.'

I traced its rounded edges and pressed my thumb against the tip, rolled and finished in leather.

'Galaad has one just like it in his size. One for both my…'

'Laurent!'

Aunt Morganne came towards us looking cross and I glanced from one to the other.

'One for both my favourite children in all the world,' Laurent finished. 'You remember what the basic moves are, Iris?'

'Attack, parry, evade, thrust.'

'That's my girl!"

'But today Aunt Morganne is teaching me to shift.'

‘I know. I wanted to see how it goes. What will you be?’

‘A phoenix with rainbow wings.’

‘Sounds awesome,’ Galaad said. ‘I’ve come to join the party, if that’s okay with you?’

‘Will you fly with me?’

‘I’ll just be watching. I don’t shift.’

‘Like I don’t do computers?’

‘Exactly like.’

‘Maurice can do both. But Gwion doesn’t do either.’

‘Ah, but Gwion understands about growing things like his dad and he’s got the best sense of direction I’ve ever come across.’

‘So?’ Aunt Morganne stood in front of me, smiling. ‘A phoenix, eh?’

‘Yes, I’m not going to change into a little fish that nearly gets eaten by a perch like Taid Emrys,’ I answered.

‘Fair enough, but Emrys was nine when he started to learn to shift and he’s one of the greatest mages the earth has ever known. Yet he still started small. You don’t think a sparrow or perhaps a kestrel might be a good starting point?’

‘Taid Emrys is Myrddin, but I’m Iris. I was Ninšubur and Shapshas. I was…’

Aunt Morganne put a finger over my lips. ‘You are the messenger of the Y Tir now, sweetheart, and very powerful. But this form could bring back a lot of memory of loss—the events you see in your nightmares, the places we visited in Greece. You'll need a lot of control to be the phoenix and we've only been studying for a couple of months.'

'The phoenix brings a new era, doesn't she?'

'She does.'

'And that's what I'm here for.'

Laurent bent down and lifted me into his arms. 'You are the bravest daughter anyone could wish for,' he said. He hugged me tight and put me on the ground again.

I saw Aunt Morganne purse her lips and shake her head at Laurent, but she only said, 'You remind me of your great-grandmother, Vivian. There was no dissuading her from an idea. Phoenix it is. And I'll be the dragon at your side. Water's my natural element so I'll be Draig-uisge.'

'Can the water dragon fly?'

'Oh, my mother The Morrigan can fly even when she's not a dragon,' Laurent said. He grinned, then became serious. 'She can be any age, kind or terrifying. She is Emrys's sister, and Artu's mirror; the keeper of death and birth. She is the phases of the moon, the power of stone and water, bird goddess, earth goddess and Lady of the Lake. She is the Great Goddess, and you, Iris, are her heir and messenger as you were to Inanna…'

'And whatever you ask of the gods is given,' Aunt Morganne finished.

And so I became the phoenix, a blaze of golden, crimson, and purple feathers, swooping over the lake from which Draig-uisge rose and joined me. I flew so high that I gasped for breath, but kept climbing. I had wings again and in a blaze I remembered everything, the callousness of the gods, the cruelties and betrayals; the thrill of rescues and miracles. I was a goddess who had survived millennia, who had fallen through myth to live again, a dizzy seven-year-old in the body of a fire bird, sparks flying from me as I climbed then let myself fall, plunging close to the lake before my wings swept me up again and I glided to the shore, a small girl, Aunt Morganne landing in the lake behind me.

Laurent scooped me up and swung me into the air. 'Brava, my angel! Brava!'

My grandfather had trained as a Druid for five years here in the ancient forest of Brocéliande. Nothing would have made my mother part with me for so long and, although I was thrilled to be learning so much, I was also a child longing for my mother and father, for the familiar comfort foods of Nain Gwen and the days learning at the little school run by Leuci and Saskia. I adored Galaad, who was two years older than me, but I missed my friends, especially Jonah and his sister, Zibah, and my cousins Gwion and Tomas. I even missed my brother, though it was often an uneasy relationship. And so my training was short and intense and after one particularly exhausting day, another when I had flown as a phoenix, my dreams, or perhaps I should say nightmares, changed.

I saw my father riding a dragon, the rhythmical wing-beats lifting him over a battle-field, close enough to hear the din of metal on metal and metal on bone. The banshee howls of pain as flesh pitted itself against steel made him recoil and I could sense his nausea. On the ground, the clay was glutinous with blood and there was a tang like rusted iron, so that he could hardly breathe for it.

The dragon spoke to him. 'The years after you defeated Hengst were good years, Artu, but the seeds of betrayal had already been planted.'

The dragon flew above a tiny cottage where a young woman was grinding herbs outside, chanting as she worked. She reminded me of Maurice, the same oval face, the same straight dark hair. She looked up and I saw my father shiver, but the dragon landed and the young woman smiled. 'You must be hungry after losing your way,' she said. It was a kind thing to give a stranger food, but I woke screaming, 'No!' and all the next day I couldn't shake the feeling that I'd seen the beginning of something terrible.

The dream came again on other nights. Aunt Morganne would only say that sometimes the story took different turns and we must hope that this would be one of those times, but I saw that she was shaken and, for a moment, my great-aunt looked old.

On my last night in Brocéliande the nightmare changed again, a jumble of images of dead and dying crops in Taid Geraint's garden and the fields and polytunnels around the village segued into images of a huge square building with a narrow entrance that twisted through various security checks, each one enclosed. I surfaced and felt a weight of grief, lying awake until the sky was beginning to lighten, before falling into another nightmare of bloody battle. Like the one I'd seen my father watching, this was an ancient fight. The grating clang of metal on metal and shrieks of those wounded and dying were this time drenched in fierce hail and rain so that mud and blood ran together. And there in the midst of the melée, in a narrow trough of mud between two outcrops of rock, were my cousin Gwion, older but clearly recognisable, and my father, parrying a heavy sword against a figure with his back to me—a slender young man with straight dark hair who lunged as Artu slipped in the mud, a fraction of a misstep as his assailant's blade slid under his guard and deep into his body.

I woke screaming, surrounded by Elaine, Laurent, Galaad and Aunt Morganne.

'Sh, darling, sh. It's over now.' My aunt sat on the bed beside me stroking my head.

'I'll make tea,' Elaine said.

Laurent crouched beside the bed, his hand on my arm. 'Do you want to tell us about it?'

I shook my head, but said, 'It's a twisted enclosure.'

Aunt Morganne blanched. 'Another battle?'

'Yes, but home as well. All the crops were dying and another place—like a big office but the entrance was odd—a twisted enclosure—and in the battle, when… when… it was between rocks, narrow and…'

I began to sob again and my aunt rocked me till I had no energy left for tears and Elaine returned with chamomile tea and honey to soothe me to sleep.

'Camlann,' Laurent said to his mother and she nodded. 'It means "crooked enclosure".'

'And the crops,' Galaad added. 'As the land goes so goes its king.'

Myrddin Emrys

Coming home is often a strange thing, especially when we have been changed. Iris left for Brocéliande a seven-year-old child, intelligent, gifted, but not in possession of her powers. She returned in the autumn, the messenger of Y Tir, not only able to travel by the power of her mind, but with the power to shape shift and with the curse of prophecy that has driven me insane in more than one lifetime. She returned with her memories and with a seriousness I would not wish on any child, but I also saw a steel in her, and a fire that would not be quelled. She reminded me so much of my beloved Vivian, something Morganne commented on too.

Gwen made a great fuss of her and, despite all that Iris was carrying in her heart and in nightmares, she went back to the little open school. Leuci ran the school in the way her great grandmother, Angharad, had. And I knew that just as Angharad had made space for me, a precocious outsider in Y Tir, Leuci would do the same for Iris. But in the hours outside school, once again I had an apprentice, one more brilliant even than Vivian, more magical than even her mother, though Iris persisted in shunning computers and maths.

Instead, she followed Geraint, Owain and Gwion

around the garden, or Osain into the forest, learning every name of every plant and cultivating her own patch of herbs. She pleaded with Gwen to begin teaching her herbalism, delighting in any recipe that used orris root, especially a cough tincture that she made with orris, ground ivy, nettle, plantain, red clover and poppy, and a salve that was good for burns, for aching muscles and to soothe an upset stomach.

The Druids insisted it took almost twenty years to train the next generation. Alys could cast equations as quick as me or summon up spells in binary that would make the greatest computer wizard pause in admiration by the age of twelve. And now her daughter, almost eight, was fast becoming an adept, both as a healer and a prophet. And, unlike her mother or me, she had a taste for debate to match her insights and skill. An heir to my son, though I did not want to think of that day.

11

September 2101

Over time, the memories and nightmares of Mount Olympus surfaced more rarely in my sleep, but dreams of doom or premonition became more frequent. Sometimes I would see something that would help Moriaen on his quest to infiltrate the Hunter empire. Often the dreams were of my father's meeting with Maurice's mother, Katie—in this life or in past iterations of their story. Once, when I was about ten, I woke from one of those dreams to see a figure standing over me. I screamed and Maurice hissed, 'Leave my mother in peace, bulb-girl. You don't belong here. This is my story and this time…'

Then the door was opened and my mother was in the room.

'Another nightmare?'

'She's fine now,' Maurice said.

'Thank you, cariad.'

Maurice grinned at me. 'Sleep well now, Iris,' he said before leaving the room.

At other times I'd dream again of what Laurent and Aunt Morganne had called Camlann. I knew the story. We all did, but we all nurtured the hope that in this life the story would have a different end. The stories are never certain. There were so many versions and in several Artu was wounded but carried to Avalon by Morganne to be healed.

I'd drift to sleep, telling myself a different story.

With the blood of menstruation, the dreams abated. My sleep became deeper and easier, but instead I began falling into waking reveries, not of Maurice's mother or of the horrors of Camlann, but of the wounded Earth. Despite ecological advances like learning how to use fungi to ingest oil spills or eat plastic wastes, or moving to cellulose plastics and biofuels, our species had gone on depleting the earth like ravenous children who could never have enough. The strides forward made in the twenty-first century were made only to be reneged on over and over again. The losses of land to the sea had changed the shape of the planet in the last part of that century. Australia became uninhabitable, many inhabited islands vanished or shrunk, and whole swathes of land around the globe were so scorched after deforestation that many areas were abandoned. Refugees from these places were rarely welcomed and tens of thousands died trying to make their way to safer places that shut their borders.

Yet in this unstable system of collapsing regimes, splintering countries and mega-corporations with more power than governments, the demand for resources to fuel the growing number of new and better implants was insatiable.

'Iris, you're miles away, cariad.'

I looked up, barely making sense of my surroundings.

'Is it your period?'

I nodded. 'Nain gave me mugwort for the pain. It helps a lot but it's...'

'Taking your mind somewhere else,' Mam finished for me.

'Not just my mind. It's like—I'm completely somewhere else. Underground actually, though that's not quite right. It's...I think I'm the messenger of the earth, not just the ground. Not just this land, Y Tir, but the Earth.'

'Negesydd y Ddaear as well as negesydd Y Tir,' Mam said. 'It makes sense, but it's a lot for you to carry.'

'It's got more intense recently. When I'm bleeding it's as though I feel the whole body of the world bleeding—as though we're one body. Sometimes the pain's unbearable—I'd stopped having the dreams about being exiled from Olympus ages ago, but now I get the burning, searing sensation in my abdomen that reminds me of my wings being ripped off.'

'Oh, Iris!' Mam put her arms round me and held me tight.

I sank into her for a while. 'Don't worry, Mam. I'm strong. It's weird and the pain can be terrible, but it's… it's a privilege as well. Does that sound mad?'

'No, cariad, it doesn't. And you're right—some burdens are also gifts. Paradox is basic to most of our lives, I think. And yes, you're incredibly strong, but I'd still give anything for my darling girl not to have to go through this.'

'But I couldn't give it up. It's what I'm here for.'

She smiled despite the tears I could see welling in her eyes. 'Anything I can get you right at this moment?' she asked.

'I think I'm going to walk down to the woods, sit a while looking at the lake and listen.'

'Should someone go with you?'

'No, but you can send out a search party if I'm not back for dinner.'

I'd said it jokingly, but she bit her lip and nodded.

At the lake, I sat on a low stone where the trees thinned along the shore. It was a warm day, early autumn, and the scent of the wind was changing after summer. I bent down and put my hands on the earth. 'Tell me,' I said out loud.

And I was deep in the Earth, her belly oozing not blood

but metals—Gold, Palladium, Platinum, Silver, Zinc, Copper, Cobalt, Nickel. And not only metals but all the elements being consumed by the frenetic manufacture of implants and the technology around them—the Earth chanted her losses as they bled from her—Silicon, Magnesium, Radium, Barium, Niobium, Osmium, Cobalt, Manganese, Titanium, Hafnium, Tungsten, Germanium, Gold, Silver, Copper, Mercury, Bismuth, Gallium, Zinc, Iron, Sulfur, Phosphorus, Cadmium, Palladium, Tantalum, Platinum, Aluminum, Carbon, Lead, Nickel, Boron, Chromium, Terbium, Potassium, Francium, Cesium, Sodium, Lithium, Indium, Calcium, Nitrogen, Oxygen, Cadmium, Arsenic, Chlorine, Helium, Neodymium, Selenium, Tin. The chant became louder and I felt the blood-flow of my period increasing—Silicon, Magnesium, Radium, Barium, Niobium, Osmium, Cobalt, Manganese, Titanium, Hafnium, Tungsten, Germanium, Gold, Silver, Copper, Mercury, Bismuth, Gallium, Zinc, Iron, Sulfur, Phosphorus, Cadmium, Palladium, Tantalum, Platinum, Aluminum, Carbon, Lead, Nickel, Boron, Chromium, Terbium, Potassium, Francium, Cesium, Sodium, Lithium, Indium, Calcium, Nitrogen, Oxygen, Cadmium, Arsenic, Chlorine, Helium, Neodymium, Selenium, Tin. Blood ran down my legs and my head swam. I slipped from the rock and sat on the earth, hugging my knees to my chest and rocking as something liverish slipped from my womb and a new chant began—seventeen rare earth elements being mined to extinction—dug out by slave labour in China, Brazil, Russia, Vietnam—Cerium, Dysprosium, Erbium, Europium, Gadolinium, Holmium, Lanthanum, Lutetium, Neodymium, Praseodymium, Promethium, Samarium, Terbium, Thulium, Ytterbium, Yttrium and Scandium. I could feel my temperature falling but couldn't move—the din of the chant repeating as more blood flowed from me—Cerium, Dysprosium, Erbium, Europium, Gadolinium, Holmium, Lanthanum, Lutetium, Neodymium, Praseodymium, Promethium, Samarium, Terbium, Thulium, Ytterbium, Yttrium and Scandium. This is my Blood. This is my Silicon, Radium, Magnesium, Cerium, Blood, Barium, Niobium, Dysprosium, Bones, Erbium, Osmium, Cobalt, Manganese, Europium, Body, Titanium, Hafnium, Gadolinium, Marrow, Tungsten, Germanium, Gold, Holmium, Lymph, Silver, Copper, Mercury, Lanthanum, Skin, Bismuth, Gallium, Lutetium, Nerves, Zinc, Iron, Sulfur, Neodymium, Gut-flora, Phosphorus, Cadmium, Palladium, Praseodymium, Head-brain, Tantalum, Platinum, Promethium, Heart, Aluminum, Carbon, Lead, Samarium, Fat, Nickel, Boron, Chromium, Terbium, Hormones, Potassium, Francium, Cesium,

Thulium, Liver and Kidneys, Sodium, Lithium, Indium, Calcium, Ytterbium, Lungs, Nitrogen, Oxygen, Cadmium, Yttrium, Veins and Arteries, Arsenic, Chlorine, Helium, Scandium, Muscles, Neodymium, Selenium, Tin, Womb bleeding elements, Womb bleeding… This is my Blood, is my Blood, my Blood, Blood, Blood, Blood, Bl…

'Iris!'

'Blood. This is…' My voice raw as stone, not mine, her voice and my blood pouring into the earth by the lake.

'Iris!'

There was no meaning in the sounds around me, only her voice becoming babble of lake and blood.

And I remembered—all of it and nothing.

And I did not remember.

There was nothing.

Soon I would return to the earth.

Return to the darkness, earth pulsing through me, blood pouring from me.

Morganne

And so my darling niece stepped into her power, our mother Earth drinking Iris's blood as she shared her pain with her messenger. I saw Alys age overnight. She had lost Brân eighteen years before and with him she had lost a part of Luke. Though they became close again, the scar tissue ran deep and she faced it each day, raising Maurice as her own. I think to lose Iris would have been the end of her, but Iris was with us for a purpose. When this part of the story ended, when Artu's part was done, it would be Iris who would be the one still standing her ground, messenger of Y Tir, messenger of the Earth herself; the one who the gods could not refuse and who would herald a different world. So young and as old as myth.

12

December 2101

Hengst Futures' Final Collapse

Iwan Jones, formerly known as Iwan Tigaen was arrested today in Birmingham following revelations of wholesale corruption in the former Connexion's giant. Jones's grand-nephew, Rick Phillips, a former government minister and son of the late Ros Phillips, who committed suicide following a previous scandal, was also taken into custody. Several other high-level employees were also arrested, including Jones's son, Sebastian Jones.

The Regulators are to issue a statement at a press conference later today, but it is understood that major irregularities were brought to light by Bradley Hunter, son of Hunter Transense's founder, Harrison Hunter, during negotiations to set up a programme of corporate global collaboration in the field of Connexions. Mr Hunter became suspicious when a high-level programmer on his team, known only as M, made discoveries during deep information-sharing and immediately reported his findings.

It is believed that that those arrested will be held on remand at a secret location and kept on suicide watch while awaiting trial.

Dewi swiped his screen closed and looked around the table at the other members of the Gader.

'So now we have a single enemy to concentrate on,' Emrys said at last.

'I have a really strong sense that whoever this M is, he's not merely a high-level programmer,' Alys said.

Emrys nodded. 'I feel the same. Hengst hasn't been a threat to Hunter's for a long time, but they obviously intend to eradicate anyone else in their field if they're bothering to go to these lengths.'

'So this M is someone like you and Alys, you mean?' Owain asked.

'Quite.'

'Which explains why all our infiltrations into Hunter's empire have fallen short,' Moriaen added. 'It's definitely not my half-brother's intelligence keeping us out.'

'Sorry to disturb you all, but…' Nain Gwen stood at the top of Capel Horeb's stairs and everyone around the table turned towards her.

I felt the room grow colder and watched the colour drain from my mother's face.

'She's gone?' my mother asked quietly.

Nain nodded, biting her lip, tears beginning to well as my mother ran to her and they hugged tight. Taid

Geraint, Uncle Owain, Aunt Seren, my cousin Gwion, my father, Emrys and me joined the circle, hugging and weeping.

Dewi stood and the room was quiet again. 'Anwen Hughes was the memory of this community. She was a healer and leader. She kept people safe when we were driven to the caverns. She worked alongside Gerhard Raven when we were under attack. She was wise and humble, a great spirit, and I think, like Alys and Emrys, one of those who are more than they seem and give more than any of us could ask. Solstice eve would have been her 101st birthday and that is a long, long life, but for us left behind, it could never be long enough. We are grateful for you, Anwen Hughes, may you rest in peace. And we mourn with your family. We grieve for us all.'

All those still around the table stood. 'Amen to that,' Zach said and his amen was taken up and echoed round the circle before everyone began hugging the family, offering love.

'I need to find Maurice,' my mother said when we were finally gathering around the table again. 'He's the only one of the family who won't know yet. I'll be back as soon as possible.'

The mood was sombre in Capel Horeb and Dewi seemed hesitant to restart business.

'There's a word in Etruscan,' I said. Everyone looked

towards me. '*Saeculum.* It's the length of time lived by the oldest person in the community. It's often roughly reckoned as a century and it also means the time when something is in living memory. Every event has its *saeculum.* My great-grandmother was the holder of our *saeculum.* Now we have to ensure that those of us who have benefitted from the continuity she offered become those that pass it on to the future. We need to stop Hunter to be sure we will be here to do that.'

'Thank you, Iris, you're right. I wondered if we should adjourn today but if your family feel the same, perhaps the best way to honour Anwen is to continue protecting the community she loved.'

'Yes!' Taid, Uncle Owain and Gwion spoke at once.

Aunt Seren nodded, but said. 'But I should go and check on Tomas. He's apprenticing with Gwen. He'll have been with her when…'

'You should go, Seren,' Emrys said.

Uncle Owain hugged her and she left hurriedly.

For a moment there was silence again, the room uneasy.

'And Iris is right,' Emrys finally began, 'this is our last stand against Hunter.'

'And we have no time to lose on this,' Moriaen added. 'Hunter will be in a position to buy up Hengst's stock. They may have been flagging for a long while but they've still given Hunter a competitor. Now they'll consolidate themselves, not just as the dominant supplier of implants for E-Gov, but for the global market. It's been in the wind and now they'll think nothing can stop them.'

'And no doubt they'll target any country trading supplies with the independent nations,' Gethin added. I watched him discreetly wipe a tear from the corner of his eye. He'd been quiet today and I knew he was anxious about Osian, at home and sick. 'Our own crops this year have been the worst I can remember. Another *saeculum,'* he said, smiling at me. 'By Solstice we'll be struggling for supplies. Time isn't on our side here.'

Cold flooded me as Gethin spoke and for a moment I was in another time, another place, an eight-year-old in Brocéliande having a nightmare of dead and dying crops in Taid Geraint's garden before images of a terrible battle, and waking in panic, screaming and sobbing. I remembered what Laurent said to Aunt Morganne when I told them the dream: *Camlann, it means crooked enclosure.* And how Galaad had added: *And the crops. As the land goes so goes its king.*

I looked across at Dewi and Gethin, both in their mid-seventies and tired, at my Taid, just a few years younger. We needed their experience and their long memories, but this fight would be brutal.

Dewi nodded as though he was reading my thoughts,

or perhaps I was adding my thoughts to his own. 'This may seem an odd time for this, but before we make what may be the most important decisions about keeping Y Tir safe that we've ever faced, I think we should think about a different leader for the Gader.'

He let the chorus of dissent run around the room for a while then waved for the gathering to be quiet. 'I've been doing this a long time. Me and Geraint and Geth hope to be the next memory-keepers of this community, but there's a lot of experience amongst us and I think we should have a leader of the Gader who has the energy for the next stage.'

'Will Cei follow after you?' Kyle asked.

Cei shook his head. 'I'm a foot soldier,' he said and laughed. 'Dad and Taid before him were negotiators, but not me. If Luke really is Artu then I'm his Sir Kay. Not a leader, but I'll follow to the end. Luke should be our leader.'

It was Dad's turn to shake his head. 'Whatever my role in this, I'm no more a negotiator than you, Cei. And I'm not from Y Tir.'

There was more dissent around the table. 'We're all from Y Tir.' I was surprised this was Uncle Owain speaking. Family and birth had always seemed important to him. I watched Emrys surveying the conversation, and wondered if he would intervene or steer it at some point, but he kept silent.

Owain continued, 'If Luke doesn't feel it right to lead the Gader, we need someone who is at the heart of the maths and magic and whose passion for this battle is unassailable. Someone who is both a warrior and a negotiator. I think we can all agree that Moriaen would be the perfect choice.'

'Yes!' This time it was Zach and Claudia who spoke in unison.

'He has my vote,' Saskia added.

'And mine,'

'And mine,' more of us chorused.

'Moriaen?' Dewi looked towards him.

Now it was Moriaen wiping a tear away quickly. 'I have never belonged anywhere else,' he said. 'You know my father is Harrison Hunter and that he abandoned me and my mother in the Subs, unwilling to recognise a black son. I came to Y Tir seeking revenge against him, but what I've found is my family and my purpose. I will lead if all of you want it, and with honour.'

'I do,' Dewi said, standing and everyone followed.

I waited till everyone else had added their assent and stood. 'And I do. In the old stories of Sir Moriaen, it says of his prowess, that *his blows were so mighty, did a spear fly towards him, to harm him, it troubled him no whit, but he smote it in twain as if it were a reed; naught might endure before him*. Whatever comes, we trust you.'

And then we were milling around Moriaen, hugging him, shaking hands, none of us bothering to wipe away the tears.

We would bury Nain Anwen and keep the Solstice and then hone our plans so that by Imbolc we would be ready for the assault. It was a hard winter. Gethin was right that Hunter went into action "persuading" governments that had traded with us that it would no longer be in their interests to help the rabble who had begun this chain of renegade "so-called" countries. Food was basic and only just sufficient, but medicines almost ceased, except those Nain and I could make from our local plant allies. With these we were able to make Osian's last days comfortable, but we couldn't stop the cancer that was eating his body and he died just after New Year, leaving Gethin heart-broken.

Imbolc 2102 was my sixteenth birthday. Everyone rallied, even Gethin appeared at our door early in the morning with a beautiful wooden pestle and mortar he'd carved for me.

'Osh started it,' he told me, 'but I finished it for him. It's from both of us with so much love, cariad.'

We hugged and sobbed together and then he held me

at arm's length and held out a handkerchief. 'No more tears today. Celebrate. You deserve a day of joy.'

He hugged me again and strode to his bike. I followed, waving to him as he rounded the corner and watched him pedal away. Mam was at the door when I went back in and she hugged me without a word.

We did celebrate, despite the shortages and the knowledge that tomorrow a group of us would leave for Birmingham to infiltrate the Hunter Empire. Despite knowing that, like us, they must have help from those who are more than human. How else had they become sufficiently powerful to block our attacks with such precision?

Myrddin Emrys

An heir to my son. Artu has not been my son in other versions of our story. We have been peers or I have been his elder, but always there has been a deep bond of love between us. In this life, though, I feel myself near breaking as the story unfolds. I have broken before. Once I spent twelve years wandering and raving in the forest, out of my senses with guilt and grief. All this power and magic, and it is never enough to force the story to do what I desire.

But the story always has its twists. I didn't foresee Iris. I still wonder if her arrival here was fate or an extraordinary accident. To fall out of myth and find yourself being the one who makes sense of another myth is not something I've encountered in any lifetime. I am used to my apprentices outgrowing me, but even my darling Vivian did not do it in a way that matches this girl. I think she may yet save Y Tir, but I do not know whether she can save my son, or me, her grandfather.

And this heir to my son has had only intimations of her own power. She is adept in shapeshifting and healing. She is the messenger of the Earth as well as of Y Tir. But I think she cannot have begun to sense the enormity of her gifts, a knowledge that will be thrust on her soon.

13

February 2102

The energy in the room in Birmingham was febrile. Tomorrow Gwion, Moriaen and my father would begin work at Hunter's, posts they'd landed posing as high-level coders from the now dissolved Hengst Futures, bringing the last dregs of inside information with them. My father would be in constant mind-link with Emrys, Gwion with my mother and Moriaen with me, though in Moriaen's case he would be doing his own maths and I sensed some magic awaking in him too. I would be feeding the gathered information back to Y Tir, my most intense period of shifting between forms and places. Although our three insiders had high-level jobs they would be on probation and we were certain that Hunter had at least one person as powerful as Emrys and my mother, who was protecting their most sensitive data. So Emrys and Moriaen had agreed that the mission would be slow and careful with the aim of getting promotions and higher access.

At the end of the first day we were all giddy with the relief that no one had been exposed, a feeling that intensified after a week, then a month, especially when

Moriaen was offered a more senior position. It was easy to be a messenger of good news as I travelled between Y Tir and Birmingham, but the nightmare of the failing crops and the terrible battle was with me constantly and at home Taid and Gethin told me the next crops were struggling again and Nain was almost completely starved of all but her herbal medicines.

Midway through March, Hunter's launched another recruitment drive. Their empire seemed to be expanding daily and Maurice began to petition Mam and Emrys to let him apply. He was bored at home and had no interest in helping either Taid or Nain with their work. They refused, so Maurice began his campaign with Dad and Moriaen. I wondered if his successful campaign to join us had been persuasion or enchantment, but said nothing. My dad and Moriaen were glad of the prospect of more help. Maurice had become as powerful a mathematician as anyone else in the team and when he applied to Hunter's he shocked us all by landing the most senior position of anyone in our group, joining us early in May when the hawthorn was beginning to blossom in the park surrounding the Hunter Transense building.

May 17 was the day of the new moon, and would be a dark night. I'd just returned from Y Tir and was in my bedroom at our Birmingham apartment, resting. In the main room Emrys, Mam and Kyle were working. Mam and Emrys kept in touch with Dad and Gwion and Kyle had joined us to help interpret the increasing amounts of data we were accruing. I was aware of Maurice and Moriaen, who I was mind-linked to, as they worked in Hunter's, but they were quieter links. Neither of them needed technical support and I drifted into a half-awake dream, but jolted awake to Maurice's voice.

'This is my story and this time I win.'

I had heard those words before, though last time he hadn't finished the sentence.

'What do you mean?' Had I heard him or dreamt him. I sat up. 'Maurice?'

'Yes, bulb-girl?'

'Don't call me…'

'Shut up and listen. I want you to know that I've been working for Hunter for years…'

'What? You…'

'I said listen. It was me who brought down Hengst Futures.'

'But Iwan was your great uncle and Rick Phillips…'

'Will you just listen!'

A searing pain shot through my head and I felt a wave of nausea.

'Yes, my wonderful family who abandoned my mother when she was no more use to them. Reduced her to poverty in the Subs so she couldn't look after me, so I had to come and live with your insufferable smug mother and my cowardly, ridiculous father. I told her to take me to them. She couldn't do much else. And I told her one day I'd get revenge. Against the Hengst empire, against Luke, against anyone who'd ever betrayed her or got in our way. You know—you were the only one who I thought might see through me, but you're weak, still living on your emotions like you did on Mount Olympus. Sentimentality makes you stupid. Maybe your vile great aunt could have intervened, but Morganne wasn't around enough, stupid old witch.'

'Maurice, you're family. You're…'

'I'm not Maurice. My name's Medraut. Mordred in some of the stories. You've always refused to admit what you knew and now it's too late. You should say bye to Moriaen while you can. But don't think you can save any of them.'

The link was severed at the same moment as Moriaen screamed into my mind with such ferocity I vomited. Mam and Emrys were in the room, Kyle behind them. 'It's started,' I looked into my grandfather's face. 'Camlann.'

I saw my mother's colour rise then disappear as she looked frantically from me to Emrys. 'We have to save them. Maurice has betrayed them. Moriaen is hurt, he might be… We need to go now.'

'Kyle, get there as soon as you can. Don't try to enter the building.'

I saw my mother touch the ruby of her ring and then she was gone from the room. My grandfather became a sparrow and I flew as a firefly, calling on Aunt Morganne as we flew.

At Transense a raucous alarm was sounding and the building was surrounded in a red glow. We found our way in through an air shaft. Every room was locked down and the people who worked there were crowding at the doors looking terrified. We could hear commotion as we reached the atrium of the building, a place full of narrow passages through multiple security gates. I remembered that Camlann means twisted enclosures. Gwion was on the floor near a security gate hugging a wound in his arm. He was rocking and his face was grey and sticky. My father was snaking his way towards Gwion on his stomach, keeping below the dark part of the screens that formed the security corridor while Hunter's guards scanned for their prey. He was also injured, dragging a bleeding leg, and there was no sign of Moriaen. I watched as my mother appeared in the security channel next to the one where Gwion and my father were trapped. The guards spotted her too and launched a volley of shots, but she had already moved into the next channel, leaving the bullets to splinter the screens behind where she'd stood a moment ago. She eased Gwion towards the door, my father following. The guards fired again but this time their bullets fell to the ground like a clatter of dropped children's marbles. The security gate shattered outwards as my mother approached it and she pulled Gwion towards the main door. The next round of bullets again fell in a clatter, well short of their targets and the main door exploded into the park as my mother approached it. I was in awe of the power I'd never seen her use before. But what should I do to help?

Emrys mind-called that he and Morganne would find Moriaen. 'Search for your brother,' he said, 'but take care, Iris. Don't try to reason with him. Just let us know where he is.'

I did a circuit of the building before Maurice called me, his voice acid. 'Come and see, bulb-girl. Come and see.'

I knew to fly back to the atrium. My mother was about to enter, having got Gwion to Kyle outside. She had made both of them invisible to the guards, though I could see Kyle encouraging Gwion to go as fast as possible.

My father pulled himself nearer to the exit as Mam came through the shattered door, but Maurice appeared from the air between them. 'This is for my mother,' he said, as he thrust a blade into our father's body. My mother howled and Maurice turned towards her, a terrible grin on his face. He pulled a gun from a deep pocket and aimed it at his own head. The crack as it fired seemed louder than all the bullets the guards had discharged. A spray of bone and blood and brain and bullet shattered the security screen at the far end of the corridor my father was prostrate in and Maurice dropped to the ground, half covering my father. I flew down to him just as Morganne and Emrys appeared from the bowels of the building, Emrys carrying Moraien as Morganne held out a hand towards the guards in their way, who fell unconscious to the ground.

Morganne took Moriaen from Emrys. 'Bring your son,' she said softly. 'Iris, we must leave now.'

I followed, mute, Emrys carrying my father behind me, my mother on her knees at the door weeping. Aunt Morganne sealed the building behind us, and there was Kyle, running towards us.

'Gwion's at the flat. He's bleeding a little still, but it's not deep. I had to come back for Luke. I…'

Kyle lifted my father from Emrys, who sank to the ground beside my mother.

Morganne laid a hand on each of them. 'We must go,' she said simply and they both rose and followed her.

At the apartment, Morganne tended to Gwion's wound and made sure he would sleep deeply. I sat with

Moriaen, who was unconscious. There was no bleeding, but the bruises on his head were livid.

'Iris…' the whisper was so faint it took me a moment to realise Moriaen had come round. 'You need…'

The code he whispered before losing consciousness was the part of the final piece to take down Hunter, but I knew it was incomplete. He drifted away from me mid-sentence. Perhaps it will be enough, I told myself, unconvinced.

'Iris,' Emrys crouched beside me as though he was talking to a little girl, 'I need you and Alys to take Gwion and Moriaen to safety in Y Tir.'

'And Dad?' I already knew the answer. I knew it the moment Maurice had plunged the blade into him.

Emrys shook his head.

'Alys is with him… with the body… We…'

'Will Kyle and Morganne take him to the Isle of Avalon?'

Emrys nodded. 'The Druid community will prepare him for the funeral. This is Kyle's destiny, to be Bedwyr to Luke's Artu. When they were young, I used to tell Luke not to get into any trouble that would affect Kyle. That Kyle didn't have Luke's protections, but in the end it's the other way round.'

'The funeral should be at Y Tir. He's…'

'There will be a memorial, cariad, but this part of the

story is not in our gift. The funeral ceremony must be performed by the Druids. Kyle must take the body to be buried in a location only he will know.'

I looked into my grandfather's eyes, but the pain I saw was unbearable. Still I needed to argue. 'But…'

'We will go to his resting place to say our own farewell. But not yet.'

Morganne

And so we went to Avalon, Bedwyr and me, as we have done before. Once the island was hidden, a liminal realm not of this world, the Tor of Glastonbury overlaying it. But in the climate disasters of the twenty-first century the Tor became an island and an ancient community of Druids took it as their mystical home, allowing no one to cross from the marshes that surrounded its waters.

No one but Artu and the Morrigan.

The barge draped in black waited for us on the shore and Bedwyr, known as Kyle in this life, found that I was no longer at his side, but on the barge—the three goddesses of the Morrigan ready to receive the dead.

His grief was terrible, but he played his part.

'The king is gone,' I told him, as I had told Bedwyr in other ages. 'Artu passes to be the king among the dead, but he will come again.'

And my brother? In some lifetimes Myrddin Emrys has been my enemy. In this life, he is dear to me, but I knew I could not save him from his sorrow. Once again he would wander, broken, but this time his surprising apprentice will be waiting for his return and she will stand with Y Tir to the last.

14

May 2102

From a high branch of a tree, I watched Kyle finish compacting the earth of the hillside and stand back. Above him the circle of ancient beech trees reached high into the sky, their enormous roots wrapping around the line of the ridge into which he had tunnelled to bury my father. Above the ridge, hovering over the trees, was a red dragon. I recognised him as the dragon I'd seen in my dream of the terrible battle. When Kyle had finished, the dragon flew down and wrapped himself beneath the trees, his wings becoming like leaf mould, his limbs and claws like roots.

'You look like the rest of the soil,' Kyle said. 'No one will find him. And you'll guard him?'

In answer the dragon opened his eyes, twisted his claws deeper amongst the roots and closed his eyes again.

Kyle stared hard at the roots. There was nothing to reveal the tunnel that led to Artu's resting place. Nothing to show that a dragon laid there, eyes closed, but alert.

'It's finished,' he said. 'Thank you.'

'We have no time for long plans,' I told the Gader. 'My

father is dead. Only the Druids can perform the ceremonies of Artu's passing. Morganne and Kyle have ensured he reached them and his resting place must remain secret. My grandmother is sure Moriaen will live, but he's still in a coma and we need to make decisions now. If Y Tir is to survive we must bring down the Hunter empire before they retaliate for the damage we inflicted at their headquarters. They will crush Y Tir in order to survive, in order to make sure no one can ever challenge their dominance again. Then they will starve all the independent nations of food and medicine and every imaginable resource. This is our moment, the only moment we have to make sure my father's last stand ends in victory.'

'She's right.' Kyle entered the room. He looked as though he had aged a decade in the week since I'd last seen him. 'They'll already be regrouping. While we wonder what to do next, Hunter will be putting pressure on E-Gov to mount a full-scale attack on us.'

Zach stood and walked towards Kyle, throwing his arms round him. 'We're glad to see you back, mate. Sit down. Tell us what you know. Was Emrys with you?'

'Emrys? No, he told me to take Luke to Avalon. I went with Morganne and she went to the island with… with Luke's body… I waited till she returned and did what she asked. I haven't seen Emrys since…'

I glanced towards Claudia who looked pale and tense. 'My grandfather is heart-broken. We have to plan this without him,' I told them. 'My mother will rally to help once we have a plan, but it's too soon for her to be with people. She's desolate. She…'

'And you, cariad?' Gethin said softly. 'I know how grief takes us all differently, but I'm worried about you. You've been through a lot and now…'

'And now she's stepping into her power. You need to listen to her. Iris is not just more than human. She is one of the most powerful goddesses ever to live amongst us.'

I smiled at Laurent who had appeared with Elaine and Aunt Morganne.

'We will do whatever is needed to secure Y Tir, as we always have. Iris is one of our own. And of course we'll listen to her. We're grateful to have you here too,' Dewi said and I felt the ripple of relief and assent run through the Gader.

'We will do what we've done before,' I said, as Laurent, Elaine and Morganne took seats around the table. 'We must make Y Tir look abandoned. This time not just unlived in. It should look as though the buildings have been torched before being left—we need to do this so that when the drones arrive they won't use microwave attacks, which would burn the houses with people inside. We have to be cloaked and convincing to their machines. We have Morganne, Elaine and Laurent but we'll need more help. We'll ask Aislinn to join us. She's well now, and powerful, and our Pictish allies are keen to repay the help we've given them in the past.'

'Sounds like we have a lot of fire power on our side. Will it be enough?' Taid Geraint asked.

'We will make it enough, but we need to secure ourselves on every front. Uncle Owain, Zach and Cei, I want you to leave for Europe. You need to ensure we have political and, if necessary, military support for our country's security, perhaps for its existence. We can't exert the financial pressures that Hunter can, and we don't have their power to bribe, but we are part of the European community and can put a lot of moral pressure on the Assembly.'

'In the meantime,' Laurent added, 'the Mutineers in Brittany are hard at work on the partial code that Moriaen whispered to Iris before he fell into the coma. Cracking it could make all this moot if we can eradicate all their digital power. I'm hoping Alys will be able to help soon too.'

'And Galaad will join your delegation to the European Community,' Elaine said.

'I can help with the decoding too,' Gwion said.

'Yes you can,' Laurent agreed. 'And you too, Kyle. Elaine will mind-link both of you to the team in

Brocéliande.'

'When the attack comes it will be worse than anything Y Tir has known before. Worse than the Winter Solstice attack that my grandmother Vivian, Aunt Morganne and my great-grandfather Gerhard Raven held off. Anyone who breaks cover will give all of us away. We've got very little time to impress on everyone how urgent it is that they all co-operate.'

Dewi nodded his head towards me. 'That's where us oldies come in. Me and your Taid and Nain and Geth. In this room we'll listen to a sixteen-year-old girl gladly, because we know you're not only right but apparently the most powerful person any of us has ever known, even in this strange place, but we don't have the time to convince everyone of this, so we'll get to work with the authority we still have left.'

'Thank you,' I said. 'I'm grateful to all of you. Emrys will be proud of us when he returns and my father will not have died in vain.'

Myrddin Emrys

No matter how inevitable something seems in prospect, no matter how doomed we seem to have been in retrospect, there is always the possibility of a different story. I have lived this possibility time and time again. I know it in the marrow of my bones. Yet each time Artu is taken from me, I falter. I have wandered in the caves this last month, but I will return to stand with those I love, with those Luke loved. I must hope that Claudia will forgive my failure of spirit so early in our marriage. Alys has taken the heavy stone of her grief and put it down quietly to return to after this is done. She has once again taken on her power as Eluned and is playing her part in saving her family and community. Iris grows in stature daily. Every one of the Gader is putting hope over mourning, knowing there will be time to grieve only if we save Y Tir.

I am Myrddin Emrys.

This is my calling and I must return to it.

15

June 21 2102

We waited a month before the attack came. Dewi, Gethin, Nain and Taid convinced everyone to go into lockdown. Food and medicines were distributed by small teams led by Leuci, Saskia, Jonah, Claudia, Tomas, Nain and Elaine. The story we told the community was that Emrys had acquired new technology that enabled us to keep those delivering supplies hidden as they moved around. The same technology was also the means to keep the houses looking deserted. We didn't say that the houses looked burnt to the ground even to drones, or that the "technology" was the tireless mental and emotional energy of Aunt Morganne, Laurent, Aislinn and myself.

My mother worked with Gwion and with Galaad and the team in Brocéliande on the fragment of code, splitting her mind to join us in shielding Y Tir for much of the time. I began to understand what Emrys had meant about her power, but I missed him and wished him back with us every hour of every day.

The army arrived at dawn on the day of the Midsummer Solstice. There were no people, only drones, faceless and terrifying. They tore through houses doing terrible damage to buildings. They burnt the crops, even though we'd made the fields appear barren, even torching the forest by the lake. There were injuries and trauma, so that Nain and Aunt Seren and a small group of doctors had to be everywhere, cloaked by Elaine, who was also a healer.

We were grateful that there was no microwave attack. None of those shielding the community had ever faced an onslaught of microwaves and it was what we had most feared we might not be able to withstand while maintaining the cloak.

At three in the afternoon the noise of the machines ceased.

'But they haven't left.'

'Emrys!' Aunt Morganne enveloped her brother and I pushed between them.

'Where have you been? We…' I began to cry then steeled myself. We were still in the midst of an attack.

'We will catch up, cariad, but first we need to strengthen the shield. They are planning sound waves, not microwaves.'

'Sound?'

'The right frequency can shake people apart,' my mother said, coming into the room. She quickly hugged Emrys. 'We will need a way to absorb the vibrations so that others aren't destroyed by them. Iris, can you keep helping with the shielding?'

'Of course.'

'And you Emrys?' Laurent asked.

'It's what I'm here for.'

'And me,' Elaine added.

'So we are seven,' Aunt Morganne said. 'It will be enough.'

'The noise could be excruciating. Lethal.' Emrys warned us. 'There are various ways they could go. Low frequency at high decibels will affect internal organs.'

'But they have to reckon with the inverse square law,' my mother said. 'The intensity of the sound will decrease with distance.'

'Which is why it's so quiet out there, Alys. They're positioning the drones so every part of Y Tir is in range. And they've also got long range acoustic devices on those drones.'

'Is this why you've been away, researching their tactics?' I asked.

'I've been living in the caves, cariad, mostly grieving, but doing some long distance watching of my own as well.'

'We wondered about evacuating to the caves, but I had a bad feeling about it.'

'Good. Always trust your body.'

The vibrations, when they began, were terrifying. They were not emitted strongly enough to cause buildings to fall. The enemy might be seeing the buildings as ruins, but they were clearly not convinced that the place was as empty as it looked. They knew we'd found ways to hide before. And Maurice had worked with them for years, perhaps showing them that there is magic as well as maths in the world. If they couldn't see us, they would burst our ear-drums or shake our organs apart.

The assault came in short bursts. We absorbed each round and each tirade of sound left the others more and more exhausted. Elaine was visibly flagging long before the attack was over and even Aunt Morganne and Aislinn looked grey and drained by the time the sound stopped. My mother, Emrys and Laurent fared better but still felt weak and my mother wondered out loud how long they would be able to maintain the cloak.

'We don't know what they might be planning next,' she said. She looked hollowed out. Her red-gold hair was limp and she seemed shrivelled.

'I can keep the shield alone if I need to,' I told them.

'Iris, you…'

'She can, Alys. Look at her. Our energy is getting sapped, but Iris's grows with every challenge.'

'Emrys is right, Mam. I've never felt so strong and alive. I…'

Another noise stopped our conversation. This was new. We felt the walls of the house shake, heard things falling from shelves, a window pane broke into shards in front of us.

'The drones are blowing up the cavern entrances,' I said. 'Probably because the community previously used them as a hiding place. They haven't been able to find anyone in the houses so they think we could be there. If they think they've sealed us in to die, they can leave.'

The machines were gone within the hour but I maintained the shield while the others rested, except for Emrys, who made his way home to Claudia. It was almost ten at night when the sun finally set and I ventured into the still cloaked street.

'What are you thinking?' Aunt Morganne stood on the step of 2 Ty Meirion behind me.

'I was wondering what they've left behind.'

'And?'

I pointed to the sky. 'Satellite surveillance. We can't drop the shield. Not yet.'

'Or lift the lockdown.'

'Quite. It will mean a lot of work still, but I've got the shield.'

'Even in your sleep?'

'Yes.'

She smiled. 'You really are something else.'

I grinned back. 'So says the Morrigan.'

It was another week before we heard from Uncle Owain, Zach and Cei. Europe had initiated sanctions against E-Gov after the Mutineers had provided evidence that Hunter had paid E-Gov to attack Y Tir. E-Gov collapsed within a day and in the political chaos that followed, a rival party that had been growing in the Welsh Assembly seized control, albeit tentatively. The top echelons of Hunter's were arrested, their implants removed.

While the politicians manoeuvred, I took the opportunity to disable the satellite surveillance with my mother's help and we were finally able to drop the shield.

July 2102

'We're exhausted and half the community is in shock,' Seren reported at the next meeting of the Gader. 'We're promised supplies soon, but me and Gwen and the other medics are working with very little at the moment.'

'Despite the arrests and collapse of E-Gov, all implants are still operational,' Emrys said. 'What's left of Hunter's is being managed by a state-appointed board of trustees. Personally, I wouldn't trust any of them.'

'We need to crack that code and disable all implants

once and for all,' Alys added. 'It's like going back to 2075 and operation Excalibur, but this time we have to block the technology globally. It's come a long way since those first experiments on people like Emrys's mother.'

'Well I know someone who can help with that.' Nain had entered the room and was smiling broadly.

'He's awake?' I asked.

'He is. A bit dazed and physically very weak, but Moriaen says he remembers more of the code.'

A cheer went up. It was the most joy I'd seen since my sixteenth birthday, only six months ago though it felt like a former life.

The magicians, as we'd become known since shielding the community, worked on the code while Cei, Uncle Owain, and Zach held talks with our new allies in the Welsh Assembly Party, now renamed "the United Assemblies Party" since they claimed to welcome alliances with the Picts, Brittany, and The New Olympians, as well as Y Tir, and supported us when we sent another delegation to Europe to lobby against the continued spread of implant technology. Across the globe, other independent nations set up their own lobbies to regional assemblies to do the same.

'It was unbelievable,' Cei told the Gader when they

returned. 'We thought we'd get shouted down with arguments about economics and progress and essential communication, but we were just the sideshow. There were all these submissions from scientists. Nearly every one of them said their work had been buried for years. Some of them had colleagues who'd disappeared. There were psychologists who'd written papers on how failing mental health went in lock step with the spread of implants and then had their careers trashed.'

'And doctors too,' Uncle Owain added. 'People like Mam who'd done research on the impact of increasingly sedentary lifestyles and been struck off.'

'And eco-activists,' Zach put in. 'The data they had on the depletion of the earth, the mining for copper, silver, nickel and all these rare metals and rare earths, was stunning.'

'And did we win the day?' Emrys asked.

Zach held up his hands. 'That's what was the most unbelievable thing of all, mate. Our great new "allies" in the United Assemblies Party have clearly already got their taste for power. They completely reneged, made speech after rotten speech on how all this corruption proves that it's vital to keep the technology in state hands from now on, never again to trust such important tools for health and communication to corporate hands, which is fine on the face of it, but obviously a smoke screen for the power to go to their own unsafe hands.'

There were murmurs of anger and disbelief and Dewi waved for silence.

'They argued for what they called a "rational programme of nationalisation" instead of wholesale dismantling of implant technology,' Uncle Owain continued the report. 'A lot of verbiage about how a modern world can't possibly function without implants so we must put in checks to ensure that future developments are in safe hands and not open to abuse.'

'And how did that go down?'

'It was decided that the Community would set up a long-term investigation by the Committee for Energy and Climate Change to determine how to move forward as modern countries with equal access to technology that neither moves history back a hundred years nor allows abuses of privacy and transparency.'

'In other words they'll do nothing and, in the meantime, politicians will find ways to exploit us again and no doubt a successor to Hunter will arise to begin the cycle again,' Emrys summed up. 'I'm hearing from other independents that the same thing is happening in regional assemblies everywhere. Schemes to "re-assess the benefits of implants following serial abuses" that won't change a thing. The process will be unwieldy and bogged down in paperwork until such time as it's hijacked or bought out by someone keen to make a profit.'

'So where does that leave Y Tir?' Dewi asked.

'As precarious as we've always been, but with an opportunity to act,' Emrys said. 'Iris, would you like to take it from here?'

'We want to launch a new version of operation Excalibur. You all know that in the old stories Artu had two swords. Clarent, the sword he pulled from the stone, was known as the sword of peace. This will be operation Clarent. To succeed we won't only have to disable all the implants in existence, but also scramble the data and computing power so that it would take an unfeasible amount of resources to begin again. We'll have help in every independent nation, but it will still be a gargantuan task. We'd like your blessing.'

'It's going to disrupt a lot of lives, isn't it?' Dewi asked.

'Yes. Societies everywhere will have to re-imagine themselves. The dislocation will be enormous.'

'But you're not doing this just to keep our bit of the world as we want it to be? We haven't just become reactionaries?'

'The reports Cei and Zach and Uncle Owain mentioned don't even begin to tell you the scale of misery that's being created by the current system. It's not just doctors and eco-activists having their lives ruined if they speak out about the problems of implants. The resources needed for them are killing the planet and rely on slave labour, a lot of them children. And wherever there are movements to stop this, they are being crushed. Operation Excalibur gave people in England a choice, but not for long enough and the dislocation wasn't enough to allow other ways of organising societies to move into the vacuum. We're not talking about bouncing the world back to the Stone Age but the rupture in the present system has to be big enough for the world to have no choice but to put the health of the planet and humanity first.'

Dewi stood. 'Then I give my blessing.'

'As do I…'

'And I…'

There was no voice of dissent.

The code breaking and maths were not my skills. If those of us who were more than human were known for maths and magic, not all of us had both. Emrys and Alys would be the maths of operation Clarent along with Moriaen, who was recovering fast. They would have help from Galaad, Isabelle and Louis in Brittany and a string of others around the globe. But the magic I would handle.

More than once it seemed that they had succeeded only for the systems to bounce back online again moments later. I watched it happen over and over before taking myself to the top of Moelwyn Mawr to think in the stillness.

Last year I'd I sat on a low stone by the lake where the trees thinned along the shore and asked the Earth to tell me her pain. She had shown me in my own body and blood how her belly was oozing metals, how her body was being carved up even after a century of floods and fires, desertification and species extinctions. I sat on an outcrop of rock and buried my hands in the slate earth.

'Please tell me what darkness we are facing,' I asked.

The sensation of falling down a long dark tunnel, my body grazed and bloodied as I fell, every bit of me a tender bruise, sent my howls screaming into the valley. When I woke. I ached, but there was not a scratch on me and I ran down the mountain, breathless with my news.

'They have their own magicians,' I told Mam, Emrys and Moriaen, who were working in the computer room at 2 Ty Meirion.

Emrys came towards me and held me at arm's length.

'Maurice wasn't their only one?'

My mam fetched a glass of water and I gulped it down between trying to steady my panting.

'This is the work of Dubh, Dother and Dian…'

Emrys nodded. 'Darkness, evil and violence.'

Moriaen looked quizzical.

'They're the sons of an Athenian warrior magician,

Carman. She invaded Ireland in the days of the Tuatha Dé Danann, laying it to waste before her sons were defeated and banished. She died in Ireland, grief-stricken. They're very powerful, but…'

'So we know who we're dealing with and they're not as strong as you?' Moriaen asked.

'Not as strong as me and the Earth combined,' I said, smiling. 'We know how to deal with them, and how to restore the land at the same time.'

Emrys put a hand on my head. 'You need to leave us for a while?'

I nodded. 'It will be nearly as hard as falling out of the Olympian myth, but I can do it.'

I watched my mother swallow hard and begin to object.

'I can do this Mam. Be ready with the maths and magic. You'll know the moment. I promise I'll be back. This year we'll celebrate Lammas in a new world and Y Tir will go on standing.'

Epilogue

On a gnarled hillside furrowed with the roots of a circle of giant beech trees, one root began to uncurl, flicking like a lizard's tail. Another root flicked free, smaller and shaped like a claw. Another followed until finally, a thick stump lifted itself and turned towards Emrys, Alys and Iris to watch them, the low winter sun illuminating their tears.

Iris reached for hands on either side of her, her mother on her right, her grandfather on her left. The shape of roots and shadows continued to unfurl, shifting from the appearance of worn bark to become the head of a huge lizard, its rough eyelids peeling back to reveal sunken pools, bile yellow bisected by slits of black. Iris held tighter to Alys and Emery's hands, meeting the dragon's gaze.

He blinked. Was there the smallest gesture of the head before the roar? The sound began with a growl, a rumble like thunder that crescendo'd to the din of a mountain collapsing, stones clattering over boulders. He flexed his wings and the air around them thrummed. His head shifted on its long neck, nearer to them, turning to gaze at the three of them so that Iris wanted to recoil from the reek of hot breath, sulphur and rotted meat, but she did not move, only gazed back.

'Here sleeps Artu, guarded by Y Ddraig Goch, the Red Dragon,' Alys's voice rang out.

That gesture of the dragon's head again before he furled his wings, wrapping himself back into the shape of roots.

'Artu sleeps!' Iris called into the wind, tears flowing as she grasped her mother's and Emrys's hands more tightly. 'But when the darkness rises again, he will return to bring the light.'

Emrys squeezed Iris's hand in response and his voice rang out. 'Artu will return when we most need him. He will return whenever people stand their ground.'

Lightning Source UK Ltd.
Milton Keynes UK
UKHW011354240223
417597UK00012B/127

9 781788 641333